RUGBY ROOKIE

Praise for Gerard Siggins' books

'Superbly written … well worth
a read … Perfect for any sports-mad
youngster'
Irish Mail on Sunday

'Brimming with action and mystery'
Children's Books Ireland

'a brilliant read'
Sunday World

GERARD SIGGINS was born in Dublin and has had a lifelong interest in sport. He's lived almost all his life in the shadow of Lansdowne Road; he's been attending rugby and soccer matches there since he was small enough for his dad to lift him over the turnstiles. He has been a journalist for more than thirty years, specialising in sport. His other books about Eoin Madden – *Rugby Spirit*, *Rugby Warrior*, *Rugby Rebel*, *Rugby Flyer*, *Rugby Runner*, *Rugby Heroes*, *Gaelic Spirit* and *Football Spirit* – as well as his 'Sports Academy' series – *Football Fiesta* and *Rugby Redzone*, are also published by The O'Brien Press.

RUGBY ROOKIE

GERARD SIGGINS

THE O'BRIEN PRESS
DUBLIN

First published 2023 by
The O'Brien Press Ltd,
12 Terenure Road East, Rathgar,
Dublin 6, Ireland
D06 HD27
Tel: +353 1 4923333; Fax: +353 1 4922777
E-mail: books@obrien.ie
Website: obrien.ie
The O'Brien Press is a member of Publishing Ireland.

ISBN: 978-1-78849-398-7

8 7 6 5 4 3 2 1
27 26 25 24 23

Printed and bound in Great Britain by Clays Ltd, Elcograf S.p.A.

MIX
Paper from
responsible sources
FSC® C018072

Published in

DUBLIN
UNESCO
City of Literature

Growing up with
O'BRIEN
obrien.ie

DEDICATION

When I wrote *Rugby Spirit* ten years ago I thought it was a stand-alone, once-off novel. But one man convinced me it was the first of a series and encouraged me to go on writing about Eoin Madden and his adventures. *Rugby Rookie* is the tenth book in the series and that is only because Michael O'Brien believed in Eoin. This book is respectfully dedicated to his memory.

ACKNOWLEDGEMENTS

Thanks as always to Martha, Jack, Lucy and Billy, and to my mother for all their unfailing support. Thanks also to all at O'Brien Press, especially my brilliant editor Helen Carr who makes all my books better.

CHAPTER 1

Although he had hardly played any sport at all in the first term at Castlerock College this year, Eoin Madden ached when he got out of bed. Happily, he no longer had pain in his ankle, which had been broken in a rugby game six weeks before.

The discomfort he felt all across his back was from the slaps of his football team-mates as they congratulated him on his shoot-out penalty that won Castlerock Red Rockets an FAI cup in Dalymount Park.

Eoin smiled at the memory. He had been out injured for the earlier games in the competition, but came on as a late sub to play his role in the triumph.

'Heeee-ro, heeee-ro,' sang his pal Alan, with whom he shared a dorm in the boarding school of Castlerock College, just outside Dublin.

'Stop that!' Eoin snapped. 'Even you did more than I did to win the Cup. I hope the junior years don't give me any of that hero worship stuff. I got enough of it after the Triple Crown.'

Eoin had been a star of the Castlerock Junior Cup rugby team, and had gone on to play for Leinster, Ireland and the British and Irish Lion Cubs.

'I signed a load of programmes for the First Years after our FAI win,' Alan replied with a grin, 'I really enjoyed the attention, to be fair.'

'It wears off, I assure you,' sighed Eoin. 'But anyway, we've a day off today. Have you any plans?'

'I was thinking we could head into town to do a bit of Christmas shopping,' suggested Alan. 'We could stop off and see how the rebuilding of the Aviva is getting on. They could all thank you for getting them jobs after you discovered the place was about to fall into a sinkhole.'

The stadium had been closed for some months after Eoin discovered one of the grandstands was on the verge of collapsing.

'That would be nice,' he replied. 'Brian might be around too.'

Brian Hanrahan was a friend of the boys who lived in the old rugby ground on Lansdowne Road – but he was not a normal type of friend. Brian was a ghost. Nearly a hundred years before he had been badly injured in a match at the ground and died later in hospital. His spirit lived on in Lansdowne Road and Brian was there to witness all of the great occasions the stadium hosted.

Eoin always got a shiver up his spine when he saw the stadium appear on the horizon as he neared the ground. Many of his happiest memories were tied to this special place and he smiled as he got off the train at Lansdowne Road station.

'Wow,' said Alan as he looked across at the stadium. 'There's an awful lot of trucks and diggers around, isn't there?'

They walked down Lansdowne Road towards the stadium shop where they noticed the grandstands at the far end had been demolished and new foundations were being put in. Hundreds of workers buzzed around the place in yellow coats and helmets.

Eoin signalled to Alan that they should head into the stadium.

'We could try to get in the big tunnel, we'd get a better view from there.'

The boys slipped inside the entrance and made their way down towards the pitch. As they were watching the construction work a man called out as he walked briskly towards them.

'Hey, you boys, what are you doing here?'

Alan turned to leave, but Eoin decided to answer.

'I'm sorry,' he replied. 'We just wanted to see how the rebuilding was going, we didn't know it wasn't open to the public.'

'It's a building site, son,' replied the man, 'it can be a dangerous place…'

The man stopped and stared at Eoin.

'You're him…' he said, pointing at the youngster.

'Who?' asked Eoin.

'You're that Madden lad, the one who found the cracks in the stand.'

Eoin nodded.

'Well, in that case I apologise for shouting at you,' the man said. 'Only for you my company wouldn't have had a huge job like this to work on. And, of course, you probably saved lives that might have been lost if you hadn't spotted the problem in time. The least I can do is give you a tour.'

CHAPTER 2

The man introduced himself to the boys as Billy and explained that he was the engineer in charge of the stadium rebuilding job. After organising a pair of yellow hard hats for them, he showed Eoin and Alan where the new stand would be sited.

He then brought the boys under the railway line around the back where men were putting tiles on the roof of a small block that had been built in the old car park.

'This is where the new rugby museum will be,' he explained. 'I'd say they'll be looking for a pair of your old boots in there some day,' he added with a laugh.

'A rugby museum?' asked Alan. 'That would be really cool.'

'Yes, I've seen some of the stuff they have to put in it, very interesting indeed,' Billy told them. 'They have one of the first jerseys Ireland played in – it was green hooped, the hoops were not as thick as your Castlerock shirts, more like that Celtic soccer team. And the balls they used were much rounder than modern rugby balls, though not quite as round as a football.'

'Is there anything in there now?' asked Alan.

'No, we haven't finished fixing it up inside yet,' replied one of the men working on the museum, who introduced himself as Simon. 'But we're hoping to have it soon enough.'

'And when will that be?' asked Eoin.

'It will open the same day the stadium opens, I think, it will be part of the whole new package,' replied Billy. 'Early next year we hope. Simon here is going to be managing the museum, so he'll show you around when you come back.'

'I'll give you a special tour of course,' said Simon, a small man with glasses and red hair. 'So do bring your old boots around!'

They walked back to the entrance where the boys handed back their yellow hats and thanked Billy for the tour.

'I'm sure you'll get a special invite when it opens,' he grinned. 'Sure we wouldn't be here at all if it wasn't for you.'

The boys decided to walk the rest of the way into

the city, a distance of about a mile. As they walked, the chatted about what they had seen, and who they hadn't.

'It's a pity we didn't run into Brian, but I suppose he would have steered clear of us with Billy around,' said Alan.

'Yeah, and I guess he's probably feeling a bit uncomfortable with all the building going on,' added Eoin. 'I'd say he'd love that museum though – he's seen most of the history in that ground since he's been around there nearly a hundred years.'

It was a crisp, sunny day and the morning had flown by the time they reached the city centre. The boys were hungry after their walk and went for a sandwich and to make plans and lists for their shopping expedition. After a ten-minute discussion they both realised that the very best presents they could get all the members of their families could be found under one roof – the big bookshop near Trinity College.

Eoin's list was short – a book of travel writing for his mam, and a historical biography for his dad. Grandad was tricky, but a helpful assistant called Lucy suggested a biography of a rugby player who Eoin knew was one of Dixie's favourites.

'He'd love that,' agreed Alan. 'Do you think he might lend it to me when he's finished?'

Eoin laughed. 'Ask him yourself. Will you come down for a few days?'

'Yes, please,' replied Alan. 'Christmas is really boring at home. I'll be on the first train on St Stephen's Day, if that's OK?'

Eoin laughed. 'I can see you now, nibbling on your turkey sandwiches as the train pulls in to Ormondstown Station.'

Alan picked up a few books as well – and a book token for his sister as he hadn't a clue what she was interested in – and the boys hopped on the bus back to the school.

They chatted about the soccer tournament they had just won – it had kept everyone occupied for most of the first term, but after the Christmas holidays there would only be one topic of conversation in Castlerock – Senior Cup rugby.

The school had a long tradition of success in the competition, but it had been more than a decade since the famous Cup had come back to Castlerock. And Eoin had got the impression from the headmaster that he would hold him personally responsible if that trophy famine was extended.

CHAPTER 3

The school holidays arrived quickly and the boarding school pupils dispersed to their homes all over the country.

Eoin's parents lived in County Tipperary, in a place called Ormondstown, while his grandfather Dixie lived nearby. Dixie Madden had been a brilliant rugby player as a boy but had decided to retire after a tragic accident at a match. Eoin had helped to reawaken his interest in the sport and Dixie was his grandson's number one fan.

Early on Christmas morning, Eoin changed into his tracksuit and trainers and went off on a run. Ormondstown was still asleep as he passed the places he remembered from growing up in the town – his old primary school, the shops, the chipper, the GAA club, and the homes of his pals. He paused outside his friend Dylan's house, but the lights were still off, so he kept moving.

Eventually he reached his destination on the edge of

town.

'Ah, Merry Christmas, Eoin,' said his grandfather as he opened the door of his cottage.

'Merry Christmas, Grandad,' replied Eoin, 'it looks like you and me are the only people up in the whole town.'

'I'm sure there are plenty of excited little boys and girls running around indoors with their new toys,' Dixie replied. 'It's not too long since you were like that yourself.'

Eoin smiled. 'I know we'll see you later for dinner, but I just wanted to drop down to say hello, and give you your present,' he said, handing Dixie the book still in its green bookshop bag. 'Sorry, I don't really get the point of wrapping paper,' he added, with a sheepish grin.

'I quite agree,' his grandfather replied, 'waste of time, waste of paper. But I'm afraid I had no inspiration as to what to get you, so I'm afraid you'll have to buy your own present,' as he handed Eoin a crisp clean banknote.

Eoin's eyes widened. 'That's too much, Grandad,' he said.

Dixie smiled. 'If you can't think of things to spend it on, then save it. You might need it if they send you off on another big rugby tour to the other side of the world.'

'No chance,' laughed Eoin. 'I'm in Senior now, and I'll be lucky to get on the school first team.' His face grew serious. 'I'm not even sure I want to be playing ...'

'I don't blame you for being nervous,' Dixie nodded. 'I'm always nervous watching your games these days. When I was playing we had fully-grown men who were smaller than some of the Under Sixteens you played against. But you do know how to look after yourself.'

'Well, I hope so,' replied Eoin. 'I'll have to start doing work in the gym and eating raw steak like you lads did back in the day.'

Dixie laughed. 'Ah, you can't be that bad – you're big for your age so you won't look too small with lads two years older than you. And aren't you due a growth spurt around now?'

Eoin shrugged. 'There's talk that the SCT get special menus up in school. I suppose there has to be some perk to it.'

He pointed to the Christmas present. 'And do you like your new book?'

'I do of course,' answered Dixie. 'I've always liked that player. Though I suppose he won't have long left playing for Ireland if he's writing his autobiography now.'

The pair chatted about rugby, and school, before Eoin remembered his visit to Lansdowne Road.

'I was shown around the new building by this man who is working on it. They have a museum in it too, which looks interesting – will you come up and see it when it opens?' Eoin asked him.

'I'd love to,' said Dixie. 'I might even have some stuff they could put in it.'

Eoin smiled. 'I know you were a brilliant player Grandad, but I think this is for the Ireland team only.'

Dixie laughed. 'Well I won't be insulted by that but no, I have some interesting items from the earliest days of Irish rugby. I was helping a friend clear out his grandfather's old house and we found this treasure chest in the attic full of rugby memorabilia.'

'Wow,' said Eoin. 'I'm sure the stadium people would love to see that – and I would too.'

'Well, I'll dig it out over the holidays and let you see. Now, what time is Christmas dinner?'

CHAPTER 4

Eoin had a great Christmas day, opening presents and relaxing away from worries about school and rugby. He had an enormous dinner and was exhausted by the end of the day, but was still up early next morning to reorganise his room for the visit of Alan.

'It's great he's coming down, I'd better bake a few apple tarts,' said his mother as she helped Eoin make up the extra bed.

'Don't be putting yourself to any trouble, Mam,' he replied. 'There's oceans of food downstairs – Alan will be happy with turkey leftovers and Christmas cake.'

Eoin's mother smiled. Alan was a regular visitor to Ormondstown and was great company for her son. And the fact that he was the biggest fan of her apple tarts made him even more welcome.

'What time does his train get in?' she asked.

'I think he said twelve noon, but he said he'd text me

when he's a couple of stops away.'

Eoin helped his mum tidy up after the previous day's festivities until Alan messaged him 'Train L8, in @ 1215. C U den.'

Eoin helped Alan move his giant kitbag from the train to the back of his father's car.

'Are you staying till Easter?' Eoin asked sarcastically.

'I will if there's apple tart every day,' laughed Alan.

'Well, I'm afraid I've bad news for you on that front,' replied Eoin. 'I talked mam out of making them today – the house is coming down with pudding and cake.'

Alan's face fell. 'Christmas pudding is the work of the devil. Don't mention it in the same breath as Mrs Madden's apple tarts.'

Eoin laughed. 'I think we'll walk back,' he told his dad. 'We'll drop in to see Dixie. Is that OK, Al?'

Alan shrugged his shoulders, obviously still unhappy at missing the tarts he had been dreaming about all the way down on the train. But he soon forgot it as they strolled along, discussing what presents they had received the day before.

Dixie was delighted to see Alan, and ushered the boys

into his kitchen where he had a plate of biscuits waiting for them.

'Your dad warned me you were coming,' he revealed. 'But I wasn't sure if you wanted tea or not.'

'That would be lovely please, Mr Madden,' said Alan, on his best behaviour.

When the trio were seated and enjoying their snack, Dixie remembered his promise to Eoin.

'I got up into the attic and brought down that chest,' he said, explaining the story to Alan.

'I think you'll have to look him up, Eoin, I must confess I've never heard of the fellow,' said Dixie.

'What was his name?' asked Alan, who was a bit of a badger on matters of rugby history.

'His name was George Stack,' said Dixie, I think he played in the 1870s.

'Ah, yes,' Alan replied. 'He was the first man to captain the Ireland team – against England, it was.'

Eoin's eyes widened. 'How do you know that stuff?' he asked.

'Because I read about him in a book – I don't have ghosts coming to tell me all about the past like some people,' Alan sniffed.

Dixie left the room and returned with an old wooden chest which he placed on the table. He lifted the lid and peered inside before carefully lifting out a green and white hooped woollen jersey.

'Imagine wearing this beauty on a hot day,' he chuckled. 'This would have been a lot heavier than the modern shirts. Can you imagine what it would be like when it rained? It would have been waterlogged.'

Also inside the box were some membership cards, press cuttings and browning photographs of serious-looking men, all of whom had huge moustaches.

'That was just the style of the time,' said Dixie.

Underneath it all, inside a brown paper bag, was a green velvet cap with a large silver shamrock on the crest, and a gold tassel.

'And this is what Mr Stack would have got for captaining Ireland that day – what year was it, Alan?'

Alan scratched his head and made a face. 'I think it was 1875,' he replied. 'But I'd have to check it when I get home.'

CHAPTER 5

'Well, you can take the box with you if you like, or I can ask your dad to collect it,' Dixie told them.

'I think leaving it here for now would be best,' said Eoin. 'I'd be afraid something would happen to it – and it looks like it might rain too.'

The boys finished their tea and thanked Dixie. 'How about we call down and see Isaac and Dylan,' suggested Eoin. 'I'm dying to know how he got on with Blooming Magic.'

Blooming Magic was the gardening firm set up by Eoin and his pals the summer before. When the other three left for school in Dublin Isaac decided to keep it going.

'Well, he's been coming here every two weeks to do a few things for me,' said Dixie. 'I'm very happy with his work. And he's a lovely lad too.'

The boys called first to Dylan, their classmate at Castlerock. His sister, Caoimhe, answered the door and had to run upstairs to wake him up.

'Sorry, lads,' he said as he shuffled down the staircase rubbing his eyes. 'I had a bit of a late night on the X-Box. What has you in Ormondstown, Alan?'

'Dublin is always boring during the holidays, so I leapt at the offer to come down here,' Alan replied.

'We were just going to head over to see Isaac, see how he's getting on with the gardening,' said Eoin.

'He's flying,' said Caoimhe. 'He's even roped me in for a few jobs at the weekends. It's dead handy pocket money.'

'Ah, that's great,' replied Eoin. 'But I hope he doesn't work you too hard,' he added with a grin.

'Well, let's find out,' said Dylan, as he pulled on his overcoat. 'I'll give him a good talking to if he's not paying you enough.'

Caoimhe laughed and told her brother to be nice.

Isaac lived in an apartment nearby and Eoin texted him as they got near to his home.

'Gr8 to hear from u, b down in 2 secs,' came the reply.

Isaac bounded out the front door soon after, high-fiving his pals.

'So, how's my company going?' asked Dylan.

Isaac laughed. 'I'm doing well enough since it became MY company,' he said.

'I knew we should have sold our share to you,' grumbled Dylan. 'I should have learned from the lads who set up Microsoft.'

Eoin laughed too. 'Ah, Dylan, will you cop on. Isaac won't be making billions out of Blooming Magic. Good luck to him if he wants to keep it going, especially given all the hassle he had in the summer.'

'Have you had any trouble with Rocky's gang?' asked Alan.

'No, not since Rocky left town, anyway,' Isaac replied.

Isaac had been abused and shouted at because of the colour of his skin, but he'd stood up to the bullies and, with the help of Eoin and his friends, he'd seen off the ringleader, Rocky.

'Good riddance,' said Eoin. 'I wouldn't mind a bit of work over the holidays if there's anything going,' he told Isaac.

'Thanks, but I think I'm OK,' he replied. 'There's just not enough growing going on with the grass and hedges. It's winter, you know.'

'That's good news,' said Alan, sarcastically. 'Here I am on my holidays and my host is looking for work.'

'Wise up, Alan,' Eoin replied with a grin. 'You came down here because Dublin is boring – well it can pretty boring here, too you know. Nothing wrong with a bit of outdoor work instead of a session in the gym.'

The boys wandered around Ormondstown, chatting about the previous summer holidays and what they had been up to since. Alan filled them in on their foray into football and Eoin's heroics in Dalymount Park.

'You must be in line for young sports star of the year on the TV next week so,' suggested Isaac.

'No chance,' said Eoin.

'He might get it next year if he wins the Senior Cup for Ormondstown,' said Alan.

'I'll be lucky to get a game,' replied Eoin. 'Lads in Transition Year almost never play in the Senior Cup.'

CHAPTER 6

As Eoin had warned Alan, the Christmas break was pretty boring in Ormondstown too. Once they had spent time with all of Eoin's friends, and his family, there was little left to do. So the boys decided to get back in shape after eating too many chocolates and turkey legs.

'There's a lot more to a lap of a Gaelic pitch than a rugby pitch,' complained Alan as they finished their third lap of Ormondstown Gaels.

'I suppose so,' replied Eoin. 'But I suppose you know the dimensions exactly?'

Alan laughed and called a halt to their circuits. 'Well, most pitches are different but even if you just count the minimum size a lap of the GAA pitch is over one hundred metres longer. So although we've done three, we've really done four, which is more than enough for now.'

The boys sat on the grass and sipped from their water bottles.

'Do you think you'll get any action in the Senior Cup?' Alan asked.

'It's hard to know,' replied Eoin. 'I'm a bit down the pecking order but who knows what will happen if there's a couple of injuries. I'll just keep myself fit and see how it goes. It will be good to learn the ropes ahead of Fifth and Sixth Year anyway.'

Eoin lay back and stared at the clouds. 'I couldn't care less if I got a game or not,' he said with a sigh.

Back in Eoin's house they met Dixie, who had just dropped over the chest that once belonged to George Stack.

'Well, I suppose that means I'll have to drop you back to Dublin,' said Eoin's dad. 'You couldn't carry something that precious on the bus.'

'That would be great,' said Alan, always glad of extra comfort.

'Would there be room for me too?' asked Dixie. 'I haven't seen my old pal Andy Finn for a while and I'd like to catch up.'

Andy was a retired Castlerock teacher who had been a team-mate of Dixie long ago.

'It will be a bit of a squeeze but you're more than welcome,' replied Kevin. 'I'll pick you up about ten.'

It was indeed a bit of a squeeze when they all clambered into Mr Madden's car the next morning.

'I think Alan will have to sit on the old chest,' suggested Dixie, mischievously.

Eoin laughed aloud as he pictured his friend perched on the wooden box, but happily they were able to find room for Alan – and Dylan too – by stowing the box in the boot instead.

'Thank you for your suggestion, Dixie, I'm not sure I appreciate it, but I'll forgive you this time,' said Alan.

'Oh, I'm sure an ice cream on our first stop for petrol will soothe all wounds,' Dixie said with a smile.

'It certainly would,' replied Alan, perking up. 'Just imagine, in First Year we were all packed into the Dixie Madden Dorm at school, and now the great man himself is buying us ice creams. Who'd have predicted that?'

The journey went quickly, even with the stop for ice cream and later for lunch on the outskirts of the city.

They arrived at Castlerock College in the early afternoon. As they passed through the gates and drove up the road leading to the school, Eoin got a shiver up his spine, as he often did. He knew he was fortunate to be able to go to such a school – he suspected Dixie must have helped out with the cost – and made sure he didn't waste the opportunity.

They pulled up outside the main entrance and Kevin opened the boot to allow the boys to remove their bags.

Out the main door came the headmaster, always delighted to meet famous old boys such as Dixie.

'Ah, Mr Madden, it is a great privilege to have you here – and you too, Mr Madden junior... and of course Mr Madden minor. And, eh, Messrs Coonan and Handy.'

'Thank you, Mr McCaffrey,' replied Dixie. 'I relish my rare visits to Castlerock. Tell me, is Andy Finn about today?'

'He is indeed,' he replied. 'In fact, he's off training one of the junior rugby sides, I believe. He has astonishing commitment for a man who should be enjoying his retirement.'

Dixie's eyes widened. 'Yes, he should. I hope he's not pushing himself too hard.'

The headmaster ignored him and made a beeline for Eoin.

'Ah, the youngest of the Maddens,' he said. 'You've brought some great excitement and a little glory to the school already this year. But, you remember our deal, now is the time to put that aside and focus on the one trophy that has eluded Castlerock for more than a decade now – the Leinster Schools Senior Cup.'

Eoin's dad and grandfather exchanged a glance. Both looked a little concerned.

'I don't expect you to play a starting role in this team,' continued the headmaster, 'but your unique skillset could be especially useful to introduce in the second half of the most important games. In fact, as I was saying to Mr Finn only this morning, we see you as a bit of a secret weapon.'

CHAPTER 7

Eoin hoped he would be third- or fourth-choice out-half, but it soon appeared that he was likely to be a bit closer to the top. Johnny Costello was the first choice, and already on the radar of the Leinster Academy talent scouts. But Milo McGeady was a long-term injury case and the next best, Kieran Hickey, was always missing training and games with various minor knocks. It was clear to Eoin that Kieran's heart wasn't in it, or he wasn't interested in hanging around to be a third-choice selection. Eoin was just as unenthusiastic, but he felt that as he had signed up he would be letting his team-mates down if he didn't put his back into it.

He was the only player from Transition Year, and the rest of the squad were all Fifth and Sixth Years. Most of them were very welcoming and full of compliments for Eoin, who was a bit of a hero at Castlerock for his rugby exploits.

They trained a lot more, and a lot harder, than Eoin was used to. Each session had a certain focus, with particular skills being worked on, like catching a high ball or working on quick offloads.

The players were expected to do an hour's fitness training before school three days a week, and seventy-five minutes' rugby after school on Monday, Tuesday and Thursday. There was a game once a week on Wednesday afternoon, and sometimes on Saturday morning too for the second XV, who were all part of the Senior squad.

It all meant Eoin was quite exhausted at the end of each day, and glad that he had no major exams at the end of TY.

'How do these guys keep this up?' wondered Eoin as he flopped down on his bed one evening after dinner. 'And some of them have Leaving Certs to do in a few months too. I'm not looking forward to that.'

'I'm sure you'll get used to it,' said Alan, who was lying on his own bed reading a book. 'And sure aren't there great perks to being on the senior team – you never get detention, and they slacken up on your doing homework, I hear.'

'But that's not a good thing,' protested Eoin. 'You don't want to leave here with a bad Leaving Cert – a Senior Cup medal won't get you into university.'

Alan shrugged his shoulders. 'It probably did at one stage. I'm reading here about George Stack; he went to Trinity and there were nine players from there on the first Irish team to play England.'

'And what year did he play for Ireland?'

'It was 1875, like I said down in Dixie's,' replied Alan.

Eoin stared at his pal. 'How do you keep that sort of stuff in your head?' he wondered aloud.

'Rugby was a mad game then,' Alan went on, ignoring Eoin's question. 'Do you know it was twenty-a-side? And there were very few rules. It must have been chaos.'

Eoin laughed. 'And what were the points then? Grandad said it was three for a try when he was young, then four, and now five!'

Alan frowned. 'I was afraid you'd ask me that. There were actually no points for a try, but if you scored a try you got a chance to take the conversion, which *WAS* worth something. Conversions, penalty goals and drop goals all counted as "goals", and the first team to score two goals was the winner. It was a bit of a weird system really.'

Eoin asked him to go through it again, but still couldn't work it out – there were NO points for a try in those days unless you kicked the conversion. What were they thinking of? And a lot more pressure on the kicker too.

He closed his eyes, but it made no difference. He sprang out of bed and glowered at Alan.

'I'm off for a walk in the fresh air. Listening to you has just given me a headache.'

CHAPTER 8

Eoin was secretly delighted when he saw the first Senior Cup team sheet posted on the rugby notice board next morning. As expected, Johnny Costello was named at Number 10, but as Eoin scanned the list of replacements he smiled inwardly as he read Kieran Hickey's name.

'Ah, Mr Madden, tough luck on missing out,' said Mr McCaffrey who was just passing. 'But I do believe you're on the standby list.'

Eoin looked puzzled as he couldn't see his name anywhere, but Rory Finnegan – who was on the team – had just arrived and spotted his confusion.

'Tough luck on not making the twenty-three,' he said. 'But we always bring along a couple of spare forwards and a spare back in case anyone gets crocked in the warm-up. You wouldn't believe how often that happens. You're our spare back, I presume.'

Eoin shrugged. 'First I've heard of that, but I expect Mr Carey will let me know the arrangements for the trip.'

They were down to play a school in Longford that was competing in the competition for the first time.

'Yeah, I expect they'll give everyone a good run,' replied Rory. 'But it's a shame you're not in as it's the perfect game to give you a senior debut. Still, you can learn a few of the songs and enjoy the crack on the bus.'

Eoin rushed off to class to tell his pals the news. Being in Transition Year they were doing some subjects that wouldn't normally be on their agenda, and Alan and Dylan were also doing Film Studies. Eoin's dad had scoffed at the idea of watching movies as schoolwork, but Eoin soon found out it was no joke.

'First of all there's no Marvel films,' he had told his dad when they talked about it over the holidays. 'And it's all talking about the camera work and themes and what the film maker was trying to say. It's not always obvious though, so it does make you think, I suppose.'

Eoin thought back to that conversation as he tried to watch the film – in Swedish – which appeared to be about a medieval knight playing chess with the devil. But he couldn't concentrate as he was bursting to tell the news to his pals.

When the film finally ended the teacher told them to spend the rest of the class talking about it with their friends and he would see them next week.

Eoin turned and beckoned Alan and Dylan to join him in the corner.

'They've put up the team for the first-round game. I'm not in the team, or on the bench, but they want me to travel in case someone gets injured warming up. Did you ever hear anything so stupid?' asked Eoin.

'Well… it's actually quite clever really, it means you can keep your options open quite late too. Didn't it happen to Johnny Sexton against Australia? If someone twists an ankle in the warm-up, or gets sick on the bus, you can rearrange things. Anyway, it's a nice day off for you down the country,' replied Alan, sniffily.

'We'll come along and roar our support,' said Dylan. 'I'd love a trip out into the fresh air.'

'Speaking of fresh air,' said Eoin, 'Anyone fancy a stroll down to The Rock?'

The Rock was a secluded corner of the school grounds, hidden by trees and bushes, where Eoin often went to be alone. It was also the place where he usually met up with Brian.

Alan and Dylan agreed to tag along so the trio strolled off together in the direction of The Rock.

They clambered through the bushes and undergrowth to reach the boulder where Dylan climbed up to sit on top.

'Do you think they'd give me a try-out for the Seniors?' he wondered aloud. 'I know they never pick guys from TY – present company excepted – but now Eoin has broken through they might want to look at some other stunning talent from our year.'

Eoin nodded, not wanting to get into a discussion like that with Dylan, who could be very grumpy if he didn't get his own way.

'I'll mention it to Ross,' he replied.

'I wonder will Brian be around?' said Alan.

'I wonder indeed,' came a voice from behind The Rock.

'Brian!' the boys all said together as their ghostly friend stepped out into the clearing.

CHAPTER 9

'So, Brian, where have you been hiding?' asked Alan. 'We called into Lansdowne Road hoping to see you, but you were nowhere to be found.'

Brian frowned. 'It's all a bit of a mess in there at the moment,' he replied, 'I don't like it when they change things around in there and put up new buildings. It's sometimes hard to recognise it as the place I've lived in for nearly a hundred years.'

'Well, I suppose that was my fault,' said Eoin. 'They've had to fix up the mess from that sinkhole and I think they're using the opportunity to add a few new buildings. Did you see they're putting in a museum?'

Brian looked puzzled. 'No, I didn't know about that at all. But I suppose that's a good thing, helping people to remember the great players of the past.'

He paused, before adding 'Though I don't suppose I will get a mention?'

The boys laughed. 'You're not the first one here to wonder that,' said Alan. 'Though I'm sure your great Lansdowne team will feature in it somewhere.'

Brian smiled. He had been just twenty-one years old when he was fatally injured in a match but several of his team-mates went on to play for Ireland and became legends of the game.

'Well, I do hope my old friends are still remembered,' he replied.

Eoin nodded.

'I'm sure they will be,' he said. 'I'll ask grandad if he has any idea where they might find jerseys or boots from those days. Have you come across any in your travels?'

Brian closed his eyes, and looked as if he was thinking hard.

'I can't remember what happened to all my stuff,' he told them. 'There wasn't much kit in my day, just a jersey, knicks, socks and boots which we carried around in a kitbag. We used to have a team photograph taken at the end of the season and the one we took at the end of my first season at Lansdowne was my proudest possession. I had it framed and hung over the fireplace.'

'Wouldn't it be amazing to track that down,' said Alan. 'They might even take it in the new museum.'

Brian smiled. 'Good luck with that one. I can't imagine

anyone caring about that now.'

A few days later Eoin was awoken by a buzzing on his mobile, the alarm having been set for 6.30am. He dressed in the dark, not wanting to wake Alan and Dylan who would get at least an extra hour in bed.

He grabbed the kitbag he had packed the night before and gently closed the door behind him.

Downstairs the dining hall was almost empty, with the only people eating all gathered around one table. Eoin joined them, nodding as the coach wished him good morning.

'Well, youngster, this is your big day,' said Ross Finnegan.

'Just enjoy yourself,' said Johnny Costello. 'You'll get a run out before the game, but hopefully you won't be needed.'

Kieran Hickey grinned. 'Well, he'll only be needed if you or I get food poisoning, which could be fairly likely given the dodgy sausages they serve here.'

Eoin laughed with the rest of them, but really hoped that wouldn't happen. It became a bit of a standing joke for the bus journey with Kieran asking the driver had he any sick bags, and making fake retching noises every time he saw Eoin.

Happily, there were no incidents before they reached Longford and drove into the school grounds where they were greeted with a large welcome banner.

'This is the first time this lot have played in the Senior Cup,' said Johnny. 'It looks like it's a big deal to them.'

The boys trooped off the bus and into the changing rooms where they were greeted by one of the opposition teachers.

'Thanks for coming, boys,' he said. 'We expect a big crowd today and there's quite a bit of fuss in the town with it being our first game. We'll have reporters and local radio covering it and a couple of government ministers said they'll come along too.'

A few of the Castlerock boys seemed to be impressed by all this, but Eoin had seen it all before. He had played several times for underage Ireland sides, and the Lions, and even appeared on the TV news after he saved Lansdowne Road from disaster.

He quickly changed into his gear and joined the rest of the squad out on the field for the warm-up. He kept a close eye on Kieran and Johnny, mildly terrified that they might twist an ankle and he would be called on.

From his short taste of Senior rugby the players were

huge, much bigger and stronger than those he had come up against.

But he suddenly pinched himself and told himself to snap out of it.

'Don't be so negative,' he thought. 'If your chance comes you will have to take it, so don't talk yourself into a corner. You can look after yourself.'

CHAPTER 10

Eoin took his place on the bench, knowing that he would not be playing. The feeling he had was not relief, more one of contentment having decided he would approach Senior Cup rugby with a different attitude.

Rory had been right that this would have been the perfect game to give Eoin his Senior debut. Their opponents were big and strong, but Castlerock played with far greater organisation and their long hours of training and rehearsing moves made it look easy.

'Come on, the Rock,' roared Dylan from the side-line, where the school's supporters all stood. A full coach had arrived from Castlerock and were starting to rehearse their full range of songs they used for all occasions.

Eoin caught Alan's eye and gave him a wave and through a series of signals he explained that he wasn't in the Matchday 23 and they would not be seeing him in action. Alan looked disappointed but continued to sing in support of his school.

Eoin watched Johnny Costello, hoping to pick up a few tips from the Castlerock out-half. He was impressed with how he directed his players, signalling moves like a cross-field kick well in advance to give his team-mates time to get in position. The Dublin school were thirty points up at half-time.

Eoin joined the huddle at half-time, helping to carry out water bottles to the team. Coach Carey gave the talk, hammering home the pre-match instructions and telling the players to keep things simple.

And so they did, and doubled the score in the second half as the home team ran out of steam. Just before the final whistle, however, Johnny was tackled by two play-ers at once, and crumpled to the ground. The physio came on and gave him a drink before suggesting he come off, which he did supported by two team-mates.

Kieran raced on, but he never even got to touch the ball before the referee blew to signal full time.

Castlerock raised their arms in triumph, but they were a bit half-hearted about doing so. Partly it was because it was such an easy game, but also because they were concerned about the injury to their key player.

'How's Johnny?' asked Ross as they reached the

changing room.

'He's being seen to by the doctor,' replied Mr Carey. 'They don't think he has anything broken, but they'll send him for an X-ray just in case.'

It was after dark when the buses swung in through the large front gate of Castlerock. The post-match buzz was gone and only a handful of the boys were still half-heartedly mumbling along with the school song. While the boys were lugging their kitbags out, a car pulled up driven by the headmaster.

'Boys, can a couple of you come over and give Johnny a hand?' asked Mr McCaffrey. 'A couple of big fellows, please.'

Ross and Andrew dropped their bags and rushed over. They helped Johnny out and he rested his arms across their shoulders. Eoin picked up the stricken out-half's bag and followed them inside.

'Are you alright, Johnny?' asked Ross, as they sat down outside the headmaster's office.

'I've felt better,' he replied. 'I didn't break anything, but I got a serious battering there. I've bruises on the bruises. But I'll be fine for next time.'

'I'll drop your bag up to your room if you like,' offered Eoin.

Johnny nodded and told him where he stayed.

'Lead on, so,' he said, as Andrew and Ross got him to his feet once more.

When Eoin arrived back in his own room, Alan and Dylan were already in bed. He filled them in on Johnny's injuries and sat down at the desk to check his emails. One was from grandad, wishing him luck in that day's game, but it reminded him about the suitcase full of the pieces left by George Stack.

He pulled it out from under the bed and opened the latch.

'I must call in to Lansdowne Road to see if they have any interest in this,' he said to himself, lifting out the velvet cap and running the golden tassel through his fingers.

CHAPTER 11

Eoin was still buzzing from his exciting day out, but he eventually fell into bed where he read for half an hour before switching off the light.

He lay staring into the darkness for a while and had just rolled over ready for sleep when he heard a noise from outside the door.

He sat up and listened. There it was again. A strange, rustling noise. Then there two soft taps at the door, as if whoever was knocking was wearing thick gloves.

Eoin jumped out of bed and crossed to the door.

'Who's there?' he whispered, but there was no reply.

His brain told him to go back to bed, but Eoin was inquisitive and he turned the handle of the door and peeked out.

There standing in the corridor was a pale man in a white shirt with thin green hoops. He wore strange long white trousers – like the pants American baseball players wear – and had an enormous moustache that looped around his mouth and down to his jawline.

'Hello…' said Eoin, nervously.

'Good night, young man,' said the figure. 'What is this place and why am I here?'

'This is Castlerock College and I haven't a clue why you are here,' Eoin replied.

'And who are you?' the stranger asked.

'My name is Eoin Madden, and you are?'

'My name is George Hall Stack,' he replied.

Eoin stared at the visitor before saying, 'Oh, you were the first man to captain Ireland at rugby, weren't you?'

The man's eyes widened. 'How on earth do you know that?' he asked.

'Eh, well, I read about you in a book. And my grandad…'

Eoin stopped and stared at the visitor.

'Are you a ghost?' he asked.

'I suppose I must be,' said George. 'What year is this?'

Eoin told him, and George's mouth opened, and his eyes widened before he chuckled. 'Well the last year I remember was almost one hundred and fifty years ago! I must indeed be a ghost.'

Eoin smiled. 'I have a bit of form in, eh, *attracting* ghosts. I've met quite a few at this stage, mostly rugby players too.'

'So people still play rugby, do they? It was quite a new thing when I was a young man. There wasn't much else to play, except athletics or cricket in the summertime.'

Eoin gave George a very quick summary of everything that had happened over the time since he had died, and told him some of the different sports people played these days.

Eoin heard Dylan coughing in the dormitory, and remembered where he was.

'I'd better get back to bed. There are people asleep in every room on this corridor. If anyone saw you talking to me there would be awkward questions.

'But I'm sure I'll see you again, George. It was probably picking up your old rugby cap that sparked off something in the spirit world that made you appear here tonight.'

He explained quickly about Brian, and where he hung out in the school grounds. 'I'll bring your cap down there tomorrow and see if you appear.'

'Indeed, I do hope to see you again. I'm fascinated by your stories and I would like to watch one of these modern rugby matches,' said George.

And with that, Eoin went back to bed. His mind was racing and he took quite a while to nod off to sleep.

CHAPTER 12

Next morning, Eoin confided in his room-mates about his midnight visitor.

'Why didn't you wake me up,' complained Dylan. 'I'd love to meet a new ghost.'

'You were snoring away, and I didn't want to make a huge fuss. You would have woken up the whole school.'

Dylan grumped at that, but found it hard to disagree with Eoin.

'Anyway, I told him about Brian and The Rock, and suggested we meet him down there later,' added Eoin. 'If I bring his cap with me, he might show up.'

Eoin carefully tucked the delicate old cap into a plastic bag and stowed it in a pocket of his rucksack before heading off to classes.

After school, Eoin bumped into Ross, who reminded him there was a special training session for the Senior squad before breakfast the following morning.

'And it looks like you might be getting some minutes against Blackstones,' he whispered to him. 'Johnny's struggling a bit and mightn't be back for the next game.'

Eoin nodded. 'No problem, I'll be ready,' he told him before wandering off to meet his pals.

He didn't let them know about Johnny, reckoning Ross's whisper was a signal that the news was not to be spread around. Not that there were any Blackstones spies studying in Castlerock, of course.

The trio strolled across one of the rugby pitches and down towards the outer edge of the school grounds. A tiny stream followed the boundary, babbling towards a cluster of bushes before it made its way to the sea a hundred metres or so beyond the school gates.

The cluster of bushes was where the boys were headed, and Eoin coughed as he pushed through into the clearing.

'Hello, Eoin,' said Brian. 'Your cough is a great idea, just in case some First Years decide to go exploring and I give them the fright of their lives.'

'Like we were when we called down here first?' laughed Eoin as Alan and Dylan followed him over to

The Rock.

'Well, it took you long enough to realise I was a ghost, so it was no shock to you,' chuckled Brian. 'But what has you down here today?'

Eoin explained to him about the night-time visitor and how he had suggested The Rock as a meeting place.

'I hope you don't mind us butting in, Brian,' said Alan.

'Not at all,' he replied. 'I'm glad of friendly company now and again. It can be a bit lonely not being seen by anyone. Maybe this George fellow will remember things about the Dublin I knew.'

'Well, he died about fifty years before you did, so that's unlikely,' said Alan.

Eoin opened his bag and took out the ancient cap.

'This was his,' he told Brian. 'He was Ireland captain that day, but he never played again.'

'It's one cap more than I won,' sighed Brian. 'Though my brother Charlie did collect quite a few.'

'And who was this fellow Charlie,' said a new voice as its owner stepped out from behind The Rock.

'Hello again, George,' said Eoin. 'These are my friends Alan and Dylan, and the player I was talking about, Brian.'

George greeted them all with a nod. 'I understand you are usually to be found in Lansdowne Road,' he said to Brian. 'That ground was just opened when I was playing rugby football,' he added.

'Really?' asked Dylan.

'Yes, it wasn't built as a rugby ground at all. It was an athletics club – the Champion Club they called them-selves – and they set up the Lansdowne rugby club to keep their members fit in the winter.'

'And did you play for Lansdowne?' asked Alan.

'No, I was at the university and played there,' George replied. 'I had rooms in Trinity College and it was very convenient to live, study and play in the one place. But I played a few matches out there. It was outside the city – Dublin was a lot smaller then.'

'Was rugby very different in those days?' asked Eoin.

'Well, I saw some youngsters playing a match in the field alongside this building on the way here, and it looks a lot more organised. We played twenty-a-side and almost everything was permitted. It was often very rough indeed.

'There wasn't any organisation for clubs either. I invited a few people to my rooms in Trinity and we set in motion the formation of the Irish Rugby Football Union. Imagine!

'And then we got an invitation to go over and play England at the Oval. That was a great excursion.'

'That was Ireland's first international match,' said Alan.

'Yes, we picked ten men from the Dublin clubs – nine of us were at Trinity – and ten from the northern clubs. We hadn't even met each other before the game!'

'Did you win?' asked Brian.

'Oh no, they were much too powerful for us – and we had no idea how to play as a team. They won by two goals to nil.'

'And was that your last game?' asked Dylan.

'It was indeed. We played England at home later that year, but I was injured and missed out. They never asked me again.

'And was that played in Lansdowne Road?' asked Eoin.

'Ah, that's a good question,' chuckled George. 'No, they didn't think that place was suitable, so they played it out in the Leinster Cricket Ground in Rathmines. But they played the next one in Lansdowne Road and as far as I understand they've been there ever since.'

CHAPTER 13

eorge picked up the rugby cap from where it lay upon The Rock.

'Ah, this all seems so very long ago,' he said, with a faint smile.

'My grandad gave me a box of your stuff – an Ireland jersey, some membership cards and notebooks. I was thinking of donating them to the new museum at Lansdowne Road,' said Eoin.

'Do you think they would be interested in it?' asked George. 'I can't imagine anyone would even know who I was.'

'It might surprise you to know that they do,' replied Alan. 'There's a room in the new stadium which has a photograph of every man who ever captained Ireland. You're there, first in the row!'

George smiled. 'Well that is very nice to hear. I must try to get over there to see it. Could I get a look at those other things too, please, before you hand them over?' he asked Eoin.

'Of course,' he replied. 'Will you come up to the dorm tonight – not as late as last night though, please!'

'Yes indeed – perhaps you could give the cap a rub when you think the time is right,' George replied.

After homework, the boys ate dinner together in the large dining hall. Eoin remembered there was training next morning so he turned down the second helping of chips the cook offered him.

'I'll have them if that's OK,' said Dylan over the hum of conversation, 'I'm taking a year off rugby.'

The cook laughed. 'Sure there's not a pick on you anyway. We'll need to build you up for next year.'

Dylan grinned as he tucked in once more. 'I don't know if I could handle those early morning training sessions,' he said. 'I'm not a morning person and doing anything physical before I eat would make me very grumpy indeed.'

Alan laughed. 'I'm glad we won't have to see that. You're grumpy enough in the mornings anyway.'

Dylan changed the subject. 'Can we come along to

meet George tonight?' he asked Eoin.

'I suppose so,' said Eoin. 'Hopefully, he'll come into our room to see the jersey and stuff. Which reminds me, I had better pack a kitbag for the morning – I'm not too great at those early starts either.'

Later, up in their room, the boys were sitting around talking about this and that when Eoin yawned.

'Time for bed, I think,' he said. 'Which means we have to get this visit from George over with now.'

He washed his hands at the sink before he pulled the suitcase out from under the bed, lifted it up on to the desk and snapped it open to reveal the treasures inside.

'They're so old,' said Alan. 'You have to be really careful handling them in case they fall apart.'

Eoin nodded. 'I try to handle them as little as possible, and make sure my hands are clean.'

'Just imagine,' said Alan. 'He wore these in the very first match Ireland played. There has been more than seven hundred since.'

'It's really thick wool too,' said Dylan. 'It must have been very heavy if it rained – and itchy too.'

'It certainly was very itchy,' announced George, who

had just appeared beside Eoin's bed.

The ghost picked up his old jersey and then pointed at Alan, who was wearing a modern green Ireland shirt.

'It's hard to believe that they mean the same thing, isn't it?' George asked. 'It really did not seem such a big deal back in 1875,' he admitted.

'Well, rugby has turned into a huge worldwide game now. These days Ireland play countries that probably did not even exist when you were playing,' said Alan. 'You would be amazed at the places where it's popular, like Japan, New Zealand and Argentina.'

'You seem to know an awful lot about it,' said George. 'You must tell me about what has happened to get from this…' He pointed at the hooped jersey '…to this,' as he pointed at Alan.

'I'd love to,' said Alan. 'But we wouldn't have time tonight. Maybe someday down at The Rock?'

George nodded. 'That would be fine. You had better bring the old cap along, it seems to play some role in summoning me here.'

A knock came to the door, and Ross Finnegan stuck his head inside the room.

'Hey Eoin…' he started, before he stopped dead when he saw George.

'Who..? Who are you?' he asked. 'No adults are permitted in the dorms at any time unless they are parents. Are you a parent?'

'No, none of these are my boys,' replied George. 'I'm actually a ghost, I've come to talk to Eoin about some items of mine that have come into his possession.'

Ross's eyes widened even more. 'A ghost? Of who? Why?...'

'My name is George Stack, and I used to play rugby for Ireland one hundred and fifty years ago. And you are?'

'I'm Ross Finnegan,' he replied, putting his arms out to shake hands but withdrawing it just as quickly. 'I better go. I just came by to remind Eoin we have training at seven o'clock in the morning.

'Perhaps you should be going to bed soon,' he suggested to Eoin, before closing the door quickly and departing.

CHAPTER 14

'Oh no,' said Alan. 'I really hope Ross doesn't tell anyone about this.'

Eoin looked worried. 'I don't think he's a blabbermouth,' he said, 'but anyway, who would believe him if he said we were playing host to a ghost?'

'We better be careful,' said Dylan. 'Let's just meet the ghosts down at The Rock in future.'

After training next morning, coach Carey gathered the boys around for a chat.

'Blackstones won't be easy opponents,' he said. 'We've usually been too strong for them but they have a powerful front row and we'll need to work around that. Johnny's not going to be back either, so we have young Eoin here on the bench. He'll come on at some stage and as he's the first Fourth Year in an awful long time to play for the school in the Senior Cup I expect you to give him your full support.

'We'll have another couple of sessions before then to work out the moves and get Eoin used to them. Now get off to your breakfast – and your books.'

As Eoin walked back towards the school, Ross caught up with him.

'That was very strange stuff last night,' the older boy started. 'Was it really a ghost?'

Eoin checked no one else was within earshot.

'Yes. He was Ireland's first rugby captain. My grandad, Dixie, found a box of his stuff, international cap, jersey and a few other bits. He gave them to me, and I brought them up to donate them to the new rugby museum down in Lansdowne Road. And now he's shown up too.'

'And does he want his stuff back?' asked Ross.

'No, I don't think so,' replied Eoin. 'I just think he's a restless spirit and we woke him up by playing around with his cap.'

Ross laughed. 'You're taking the mickey here, aren't you?'

Eoin shook his head. 'No, but please don't say it to anyone. They'd think I'm mad. George is a nice lad, and he and Brian seem to get on well enough…'

'Who's Brian?' asked Ross.

Eoin went red, and was glad when Kieran joined them.

'Hey, Kieran, you were looking good in training,' said Eoin, quickly changing the subject.

'I'm not sure about that,' he replied. 'Carey doesn't rate me, and to be honest I'm getting a bit bored with rugby.'

'But you're first choice now that Johnny's injured,' Eoin answered.

'Maybe,' replied Kieran, 'but I get the impression that they're all waiting for an excuse to promote you, TY or not.'

Eoin was stunned. 'I'm not ready to play senior yet,' he said. 'I'd be murdered by some of the big lumps we come up against. You've been playing against the same players for years.'

Kieran sighed. 'I'll give it a go, but I've been so long acting as understudy to Johnny that my heart is not in it anymore.'

Ross chipped in: 'Eoin's right,' he said. 'You've been number two since First Year. You know all the team and all our moves. You can't pull out now that you have a chance to establish yourself as number one out-half. And you can't let the rest of the team down either.'

Kieran shrugged. 'I'll be there, and I'll play. But as soon as Eoin's up to it he should be in the starting team. He's class and he's the future. We might not win the cup this year, but he will win it for us next year.'

CHAPTER 15

Blackstones did indeed have a very large pack, and their wing-forwards looked especially rough. One of them eyeballed Eoin during the warm-up and licked his lips.

Eoin glowered back, refusing to appear intimidated, but inside he was feeling a little queasy.

He took his place on the bench and looked around the field, checking out where the Castlerock supporters were standing and picking out Dylan and Alan among them.

Blackstones started like a train, and used their powerful pack to bulldoze Castlerock back to their goal line in the first five minutes. But the defence held firm and Blackstones eventually got tired of battering away and took a shot for goal with the first penalty that was awarded.

Eoin studied his team and reckoned they had a strong

and fast pair of wings who needed to get the ball more often. Kieran was very fond of launching Garryowens or kicking for touch, which meant the wingers hardly saw the ball in the first half.

Just before the break Blackstones won a line-out on half-way and after the maul took them into the Castlerock 22, their big No.8 broke off and charged towards the posts. Kieran chased after him but his tackle was half-hearted and the No.8 romped over to score a try which was easily converted for a 10-0 half-time lead.

Mr Carey was not happy at half-time and was particularly annoyed with Kieran for his failure to prevent the try. 'You had caught him, Kieran, all you needed was to fully commit to the tackle and you bottled it.' Kieran looked down and shook his head.

'We won't make changes yet,' said the coach, 'but around the hour mark we'll shuffle the front row and maybe a couple of other changes. So push yourselves hard and let's get back in this game.'

Eoin wandered back to the bench, secretly relieved that he was not required yet, but also looking forward to getting out on the field if and when his moment came.

It came sooner than he expected. Castlerock won a penalty just inside the 22 about ten minutes into the second half. Kieran stepped up to take it but fluffed it badly, the ball slicing off his boot and dribbling over the line wide of the posts.

That was the last straw for Mr Carey, and he signalled to Eoin to take off his tracksuit and warm up for action.

As Eoin jogged along the touchline he heard some boys from Blackstones calling him a baby, and saying he would be murdered when he got out on the field, but Eoin was able to block out all the abuse, whistling to himself and turning his face towards the field as he passed the group.

At the next break in play Mr Carey called Kieran ashore, and ushered Eoin on to the field.

'Just do the simple things, Eoin, we can win this,' he told him. 'And I hope you have your kicking boots on.'

Eoin gulped and jogged into position.

Ross winked at him and told him: 'We have your back, Eoin.'

Eoin smiled thinly and waited for the line-out to be taken.

The ball was won by Ross and he fed it quickly to Cillian Browne at scrum-half. He checked out his options before flipping the ball out to Eoin. The slight delay had given the Blackstones flankers a chance to make ground but as they converged on Eoin he passed it out to the centre.

Crunch. Their tackle still arrived even though the ball was gone and Eoin felt as if he had been hit by a double-decker bus.

He lay on the ground for a second and decided he better not show he was rattled, and got to his feet as quickly as he could.

CHAPTER 16

oin rejoined the play just as Castlerock regained control of the ball around half-way.

He stood behind the scrum-half, who had his foot on the ball and was checking his options. Eoin opened his hands to signal he wanted a pass, and Cillian delivered to ball straight to him. Eoin swung around on his left foot and kicked the ball diagonally across the field towards the Blackstones 22.

Colin Greaney came haring down the touchline in pursuit and the Castlerock winger was a real speed merchant. The ball had almost reached the sideline when he raced up to it, scooped it into his hands and made for the corner, pursued by three boys in black.

But Colin wasn't going to be caught, and he timed his dive to hit the line before he was submerged in a sea of pursuers.

'Fantastic kick, Eoin,' said Ross as they ran to congratulate Colin. 'Good luck with the convert.'

Eoin gulped. As Colin had scored far out in the corner, he now had a tricky conversion on the line back out from where the winger had touched down. Eoin gathered the ball and trotted out close to the 22 to give himself the best chance on an angle. He picked up a kicking tee one of the subs had tossed his way, and settled himself for the kick.

He placed the ball and took ten steps backwards before shifting two steps to his left and pausing to look up at the white posts.

He blew out and filled his lungs before starting his short run.

'Madden, you're a clown!' came a call from the sideline, which caused Eoin to pause for a tenth of a second. It was enough to put him off his kick, and he scuffed his boot off the ball, which spiralled wide of the upright.

Eoin was furious, not just with the bad-mannered abuse from the spectator, but at himself for allowing himself to get distracted by it.

'Bad luck, Eoin,' said Ross as Eoin ran back.

'It wasn't bad luck,' replied Eoin, 'it was bad concentration. I shouldn't let those idiots get to me.'

Ross nodded. 'Put it out of your head, we'll need

you focusing a hundred per cent when you take the next kick.'

Eoin checked the time with the referee who told him there were seven minutes left.

Blackstones went on the attack and had worked their way into the Castlerock 22 when their out-half flung a risky pass which missed both their centres. He had planned to find the Blackstones winger who had a great turn of speed – if the ball reached him there was no one on the field who could catch him.

But Blackstones had not reckoned on Oisín O'Neill, who spotted exactly what the out-half was up to.

He raced out of the line and leapt high in the air to pluck the ball out of the sky. He continued his sprint and raced into the Blackstones half. The speedy opposing winger set off in pursuit but Oisín was too far ahead – the wing got his tackle in but by that stage the Castlerock centre was just short of the try line and his momentum carried him over, right under the posts.

Eoin collected the ball from Oisín and went to tee-up the conversion. Ross winked at him but didn't say anything, preferring to show Eoin through his silence that he had complete confidence in his kicking.

Ross was justified, and Eoin smashed the ball straight and true between the posts to put Castlerock 12-10

ahead. He turned towards where the Blackstones supporters were standing and gave them a wide grin and
a thumbs-up.

CHAPTER 17

The full-time whistle came soon afterwards and the Castlerock forwards lifted Eoin up on their shoulders and carried him from the field.

Mr Carey and the rest of the subs came out to meet them and it was a happy Castlerock party that returned to the dressing rooms.

'That was a brilliant interception, Oisín, and a nerveless conversion, Eoin,' said the coach. 'But you all played really well in the second half, and we recovered very well to reach the semi-finals, where we will be playing St Osgur's.'

Eoin opened his bootlaces and sat back on the bench. The rest of the players were still singing and whooping it up after a tight game and a narrow victory.

Eoin looked around the room and grinned. Three weeks he ago he was terrified about being in the senior team with these boys. He still didn't feel entirely a part of the team but was glad he was able to play his part in the win and that they valued his contribution.

He spotted Johnny Costello limping in on his crutches, and making for coach Carey. The room was noisy, but Eoin was able to pick up the gist of what they were talking about. He saw Johnny point in his direction and say, 'He's got to start the semi.'

Eoin smiled, delighted that he had impressed a senior player but still not convinced that Johnny was correct. He quickly dressed and went outside to meet Alan and Dylan.

'You were fantastic,' said Alan, 'and that cross-kick to Colin was text-book stuff.'

'Yeah, and as for your ice-man nerves for that conversion...' said Dylan.

'Ha, ha, I did enjoy that one,' replied Eoin. 'Though I was still raging about that Blackstones kid who roared at me before the last kick. I shouldn't have let him get to me.'

'Ah look, you just have to shut that all off,' said Dylan, 'Train yourself to ignore all the outside noises.'

'He's right,' Alan agreed. 'So how about we take a detour going back to school? If we stay on the Dart for a few extra stops we can visit the Aviva and see what's going on.'

'Yeah, that would be good,' Eoin nodded. 'I want to see that museum guy and see if he's interested in George Stack's stuff.'

Eoin went inside to check with Mr Carey that it was OK to take their time returning to school and gave his friends the thumbs-up when he got back.

Rather than join the rest of the Castlerock party, the trio decided to avoid any awkward questions about their extended journey and found a near-empty carriage at the back of the train.

There they chatted about the match and their chances against St Osgur's, a school Eoin had played against on several occasions in his time at Castlerock.

'They hate you there,' said Dylan. 'Is there any chance he'll start with you in the semi? That Kieran lad is useless. No bottle.'

'That's a bit unfair,' said Eoin, 'he's just a bit lackadaisical. I'm not even sure he enjoys playing at all.'

'Imagine being good enough to play on the SCT, and not caring enough to try,' said Dylan, his temper starting to rise. 'He definitely should be nowhere near the team.'

'Maybe,' replied Eoin, 'but he's got a bit of talent, even if his goal-kicking leaves a bit to be desired.'

CHAPTER 18

The trio watched as the rest of the Castlerock boys left the Dart train and headed back towards school. Eoin checked the time and saw they had two hours to complete their mission and get back in time for dinner. With Dylan this was a vital thing to consider as he could become very bad tempered without regular feeding.

Four stops down the line they arrived at Lansdowne Road and left the train. Eoin led the boys to the stadium site entrance, where he asked for Billy the engineer.

'Billy's up working on the museum,' the receptionist told him. 'I'll give him a call for you.'

'That's perfect, thank you,' replied Alan. 'It's the museum we want to visit.'

Billy arrived soon after, handing each of the boys a bright yellow hard hat.

'What has brought you lads back?' he asked.

Eoin explained about the suitcase full of George's

rugby relics and how they wanted to see whether the museum would be interested in taking them from him.

'Gosh, I'm sure they will,' said Billy. 'Let me bring you over to Simon – his collection is coming together well but that sounds very special indeed.'

Billy took them over to where the new museum stood and knocked twice on the temporary wooden door.

'Come in,' called Simon, who was hanging a giant painting on the wall.

'Anyone recognise this lad?' he asked.

Eoin shook his head, but Alan thought he knew.

'Is that Ciaran Fitzgerald?' he asked. 'The was the captain of the Triple Crown teams back in the 1980s, I think.'

'Full marks,' said Simon. 'We have a gallery of all our great captains – photos, paintings, jerseys, caps and so on. We have almost all of them now.'

'Do you have the first one of all?' asked Eoin.

'Ah, George Hall Stack,' replied Simon. 'He was a bit of a mystery man.'

'How was that?' asked Eoin.

'Well, he captained Ireland in our very first inter-national match, against England at The Oval cricket ground in London. But that was the only game he ever played for Ireland. We don't know why he wasn't picked for the next fixture, which was also held at a cricket ground – in Rathmines here in Dublin – later that year. And by the time the third game came around, poor George was dead, aged just twenty-six.'

'Really?' asked Alan. 'That's very young.'

Simon nodded. 'Yes, it's a sad story. He took the wrong medicine for a sick stomach, and it killed him. Doctors weren't as skilled in those days.

'We have very little in our collection about him – a small photo taken out of a Trinity College team group – and some family details from his home in Omagh.'

Eoin said, 'Well, what would you think if I were to tell you that I have a suitcase back in school with George Stack's Ireland cap, jersey and team photo as well as lots of other items like letters and membership cards?'

Simon's eyes widened. 'Well I would tell you first that I would very much like to see them. Stack was one of the founders of the IRFU and that material could increase our sparse knowledge of those times. I'm extremely excited to hear about this. Would you like to lend the items to the museum here?'

Eoin nodded. 'Well they came from my grandfather, and he told me to give them a suitable home. I can't think of anywhere more suitable than this.'

Simon smiled and thanked Eoin. 'When can we see

these items?' he asked. 'I can call out to your school if you like?'

Eoin nodded and said he would check with the headmaster, but the school didn't allow adult visitors who were not family.

'I can call back here later in the week,' Eoin said.

Simon showed them around the rooms that would become the stadium museum, with some of the exhibits already in place.

'This is about the very early history of the ground when it was mostly used for athletics,' he told the boys. 'We don't have many items concerning rugby from Stack's time so it would be wonderful to see what you have.'

CHAPTER 19

The trio raced back to the train station just in time to get on board the Dart, and discussed what they had seen in the museum.

'I thought the old jerseys were class,' said Dylan. 'Though they must have been very itchy and heavy to wear.'

'At least they would have been warmer than some of the ones they have these days,' chipped in Alan. 'You'd freeze out on the wing sometimes.'

'I'd love to try on George's jersey,' said Dylan, 'but I suppose it's very fragile – I'd be afraid I'd destroy it.'

They arrived at the school gates in plenty of time for dinner, so Eoin suggested they take a quick detour down to The Rock and visit Brian.

'Hello…' he called out as he made his way through the bushes. 'Are you around, Brian?'

When they reached the clearing there was no sign of

Brian, but Alan suggested they wait a few minutes in case he was nearby. Sure enough, Brian appeared thirty seconds later.

'I just got a feeling you would be here,' the ghost said. 'I saw you in Lansdowne Road earlier, but you were always with adults so I couldn't just make an appearance.'

'And what were you up to in there?' asked Eoin.

'Just keeping an eye on things,' he replied. 'I've been hearing some whisperings about strange characters hanging around the stadium and I wanted to go in there to check for myself.'

'And what did you see?' asked Alan.

'Well, the strangest characters I saw were three lads in Castlerock tracksuits and yellow helmets,' Brian chuckled. 'But there were a couple of guys hanging around outside who didn't seem to have any reason to be there. One of them was taking photos of the museum through the fence. Another had a clipboard and I got up close and saw all he was doing was counting the people on the site and where they were working. He also had a map of the grounds with all the entrances marked. They all had yellow helmets, but they didn't seem to be doing anything useful at all.'

'We had yellow helmets and weren't too useful either,' said Dylan.

'Yeah, but we were there for a reason,' said Eoin. 'We were asking the museum manager if he wanted George's box of artefacts.'

'And was he interested?,' asked Brian.

'Yes,' replied Eoin. 'He says they have very little information on George and his times so the stuff we brought up could be very important.'

'Well, look after it,' said Brian. 'Those dodgy characters hanging around may have their eyes on such items.'

On the way into the dining hall, Eoin was mobbed by gangs of First and Second Years.

'Can I have your autograph, Mister Madden?,' one asked him.

Eoin smiled. 'I'm not Mister Madden, I'm Eoin,' he replied. 'And of course I'll sign an autograph. But in future would you mind waiting for me to finish my dinner? I don't really like cold carrots.'

Eoin signed the youngster's book and promised the rest he would stay back after dinner if anyone else wanted a signature.

Ross signalled for him to join the Senior Cup squad at the top of the room. Eoin shrugged his shoulders and whispered 'sorry' as he left his pals.

'We always eat together when we come back here after a game,' he explained. 'It doesn't matter what year you are in, you have to sit at the top table – the teachers usually sit here but they know to stay away on these occasions,' he added, with a wink.

The full matchday squad were there, with coaches, and also those boys who would have been there but for injury, such as Johnny Costello.

'Hey Eoin,' called Johnny, 'sit over here with the reserve No.10s'. Eoin blushed as he walked along the table to where Johnny sat.

'Though how much longer will you be the reserve, I wonder?' he laughed.

Eoin didn't really enjoy the dinner; he was two years younger than almost everyone else and didn't understand most of the banter and in-jokes. He looked down at Alan and Dylan laughing away with the rest of his class and wished he was back down with them. He was relieved when the headmaster rang the bell to close the meal and he could run over to see his pals.

'What's it like eating with the big boys?' asked Dylan.

'It's great, we get extra chips and double helpings of apple tart,' he replied.

'Really?' said Alan, with an appalled look on his face.

'NO!' laughed Eoin. 'We get the same slop as you got. Just we had it at the top table, so we got served first, which was nice. The lads aren't bad company either – if I only knew what they were talking about.'

CHAPTER 20

A couple of days later the boys had a half-day and Eoin decided it would be a good time to call into Lansdowne Road. As usual, Alan and Dylan were delighted to go along for the ride.

Rather than lugging the suitcase along, Eoin carefully placed the items in a plastic bag and stowed them in a shoulder bag before he and his pals wandered down to the railway station.

There were quite a few Castlerock boys on board, and a few gave Eoin a wave, even though he didn't have a clue who they were.

'You're popular,' snipped Dylan. 'We might have to sit in the first-class carriage soon.'

'I'm afraid there's no first class on the Dart,' replied Alan. 'But if you prefer, you could travel in on the bus when we're on this in future?'

Dylan growled, but happily their short journey was

close to complete and Eoin hopped up out his seat and went to stand by the doors until the train stopped.

Again they went to reception, and this time asked for Simon. He arrived with three yellow hard hats and three plastic badges on a ribbon to wear around their necks.

'Thanks for coming in, lads,' he said. 'We've been busy here this last week with lots of new exhibits coming in. Did I read that you won your schools' cup match?'

Eoin nodded. 'Yes, we've got St Osgur's in the semi-final.'

'Really?' said Simon. 'That's my old school. Though we never got as far as the semi-final when I was there,' he added with a frown.

He invited the boys into his office, which was just off the main room of the museum.

'Well now, let's see what delights you have brought along today,' he said.

Eoin lifted his haversack onto the desk, and carefully removed the plastic bag.

'I'm glad to see you've taken such care,' said Simon. 'You wouldn't believe how careless some people can be with old, priceless objects.'

Eoin opened the bag and lifted out the jersey, cap, membership cards and a bundle of letters and notebooks tied up in a decaying ribbon.

'Gosh, this looks exciting,' said Simon. 'Have you any idea about what's written in there?'

'No,' said Eoin. 'I tried, but his handwriting is very weird. It's very old-fashioned and I couldn't pick out more than one word every line. I hope you have better luck.'

Simon smiled. 'Well, it is true that people's handwriting has changed enormously over the past century. But I have plenty of experience of reading documents from the eighteenth and nineteenth centuries so I'm hoping this will be quite straightforward.'

Simon picked up the jersey first. 'Wow, this is fantastic… imagine, the first men to play rugby for Ireland wore this. It's a strange design, with these thin hoops. I'm glad we didn't stick with it.'

He picked up the cap and ran his fingers through the tassel and examined the large shamrock embroidered with silver thread. Eoin suddenly became aware of a new presence in the room. He looked over his shoulder and saw George standing beside the door, although no one else seemed to notice his arrival.

'The quality of this cap is astonishing,' said Simon. 'I've seen some from the 1890s and they are not nearly as well made as this one. I suppose the idea of caps would only have started around this time.'

Simon looked at the membership cards, which gave a list of fixtures for the Dublin University club, and carefully opened the ribbon holding the notebooks and letters together.

He put the notebooks to one side, and sorted through the rest of the documents, taking out some team sheets and making a small pile on his desk.

He looked at the first letter, which was from the secretary of the Irish Rugby Football Union, inviting George to meet up at the front gate of Trinity College and from there travel by carriage to catch the ferry to Wales, and the onward train to London.

'These are amazing details,' said Simon, 'we will learn so much about the early days of Irish international rugby from them. Thank you so much for bringing them in.'

Eoin smiled. 'That's no problem, Simon. Like I said, Grandad Dixie was just keen that they find a right home.'

'We'll certainly give them a great display – there's enough here to make a full exhibition board for George alone.'

Eoin looked at where the ghost was standing and caught him smiling.

'I'm sure George would be delighted to hear his name will live on at the home of Irish rugby, and lots more people can learn more about his enormous contribution to the growth of the sport,' Eoin added.

'Yes indeed,' said Simon. 'It's just a pity he isn't here today to hear that.'

CHAPTER 21

The Senior Cup team trained all week after school, and Mr Carey kept everyone guessing by switching between Eoin and Kieran, teaching them both the same drills and the same moves.

The coach took Eoin aside after one session.

'Right, Eoin, I suppose you're wondering what we're up to this week?' he started.

'Well, sort of…' replied Eoin.

'To be honest, we're still not quite sure,' Mr Carey said. 'We're delighted to have you in the panel, but we're still unsure whether a TY student has the experience, and physical capacity, to cope with the challenges of the final rounds of the Leinster Schools Senior Cup.

'But that said, we must play with the hand we have been dealt, and that includes losing Johnny to injury. As you must have noticed the last day, Kieran is probably not a starting number ten. The fact that his goal kicking has gone to pot has not helped either.

'I brought you on the last day because I was getting frustrated with his decision-making and was very pleased that you settled so well. I am now inclined to start with you, but other voices are concerned that you might not be up to the job physically. You are a bit behind the rest of them in development, but we can work on that with the strength and conditioning coach. We are playing St Osgur's and – probably – St Malachy's in the final, so we know we are in for two tough battles if we go that far.

'Johnny Costello is a big fan of yours, and he thinks you can be a starter on the team. Johnny's on his way back by the way, we should be able to pick him in the panel for the final – if we get there, of course.'

'That's great news,' said Eoin. 'I'd be delighted to step back to let Johnny play. He's a class player.'

'Anyway, we may not decide on the starting fifteen until a couple of days before the game, which I hope you understand. But I just wanted to let you know what we were thinking,' added the coach.

Eoin nodded. 'Yes, and I appreciate that. I'll play whatever role the school wants me to play. It's all about Castlerock winning the cup after all.'

Back in the dormitory Eoin relayed the conversation with Mr Carey to Dylan and Alan.

'They HAVE to pick you Eoin,' said Dylan. 'That Kieran fella is useless and a bit of a coward too.'

'Ah that's not fair,' said Eoin. 'He's not a coward, he's a bit – as Dixie would say – "a bit windy". But it's not easy playing number ten in a senior cup team.'

'But he just gives the impression that he's not that interested,' said Alan. 'There's dozens of kids would give their left arm to be as talented as he is.'

'You wouldn't be much of a tackler without a left arm,' replied Eoin, with a grin.

'You know what I mean,' said Alan, throwing a pillow at his pal.

Eoin snatched the pillow out of the air, took it down, and passed it to Dylan as if he were Castlerock's first centre.

Dylan played along, pushing a hand-off towards Alan, sidestepping the armchair, and diving towards the door-way to claim the try.

'Good score,' said George, who had just appeared in the corridor and lifted his left arm in the air like a referee awarding a try.

'Hi, George,' said Eoin. 'I saw you earlier in the stadium, but you disappeared fairly quickly.'

'Yes,' nodded the ghost. 'I was quite delighted that my old possessions would be appreciated by modern rugby supporters, but a little sad at the memories it brought back of the long-dead people I used to play with.'

'It must be strange to be a ghost,' said Alan.

'It is indeed,' said George. 'Most of the time you're just asleep, or whatever, but then every few years you become awake and get out into the world again. And what a very different world this is.'

'Dublin must have changed a lot,' said Eoin.

'Well, the city has changed, that's true,' George replied, 'but everything else is very confusing as well. Those little metal boxes on wheels that people go around in are new to me, and the trains running down the main streets. And as for the clothes people wear... Some of the buildings seem enormous – when I was alive you never saw anything more than four storeys.

'I don't think I miss the horses in the street – I do love the animals, but in my day they made walking around the city quite hazardous as you really had to watch where you put your feet.'

Alan laughed.

'It's great what they're doing with the museum, isn't it,' said Eoin.

George nodded. 'Yes, I'm greatly honoured but also

a little bit concerned. There are some people working there who are not as honest as they should be. Last week I saw one of them slip a gold medal into his pocket. I can't imagine why he would do that in the normal course of events.'

Eoin frowned. 'I could have a word with Simon, he's the manager there. Unless he was the one who did it? Simon was the man who was talking to us when you appeared.'

'No, that was not him. It was a small, slight chap with curly brown hair. I will point him out to you when we next visit.'

CHAPTER 22

When he was on the Lion Cubs tour to New Zealand, Eoin had discovered that there was a big black market in rugby memorabilia, souvenirs of the great players and teams of the past. He told the story of that adventure to Dylan and Alan once George had left.

'The coach was in on the robbery of a trophy,' he told them. 'He knew a guy back in England who would give thousands for it. I was so happy to stop that – especially as the trophy was named after our old friend Dave.'

Dave Gallaher was another of Eoin's ghostly pals. He was an Irish-born All Black who was killed in the First World War and in whose honour the Gallaher Shield was named. In another of his adventures Eoin had also helped to prevent the theft of the William Webb Ellis Cup, the World Cup trophy.

'The museum must have things that are worth millions,' said Dylan. 'Imagine what you might get for

George's Ireland cap?'

Eoin frowned. 'I really hope Simon has it under lock and key.'

The headmaster organised a special coach for the Senior Cup team to take them into the Donnybrook stadium where they were to face St Osgur's. Eoin had played against the school a number of times in big matches since they first met in the Father Geoghegan Cup final way back in First Year. He wondered if he would be playing against any of the boys he had faced before in schools matches.

The team bus was silent as it pulled into the stadium car park. In previous years similar journeys had been full of singing and laughter, but the Senior Cup was a serious business and most of the boys were listening to music on headphones and kept to themselves as they left the bus.

Inside the dressing room they togged out quickly and waited for Mr Carey's instructions.

'It's the first time in this place for a few of you, but don't feel intimidated by the grandstand – it's a small ground really and it's the same for both teams. And remember, you have a much greater prize for winning, a game in the Aviva, which is something you will tell your grandchildren about.'

He kept his instructions simple, trusting the players had learned their roles in the weeks leading up to the game.

'But I want to give a special word for a special player. Eoin Madden is making history here and I know you will all give him your full support. Let's win this, get to the final and be remembered as the first of the great Castlerock three-in-a-row teams.'

Eoin gulped, and nodded to Mr Carey as they all left the dressing room. He got a few claps on the back, and Ross wished him luck and told him he had no doubt that he would be fine. Outside, there were very few supporters scattered around the ground, but a steady trickle suggested that it wouldn't be long until it was full.

Eoin raced onto the pitch, which was one of the modern 3G artificial surfaces. He liked the feeling running on the surface but winced remembering the burns he sometimes got on his knees when he fell on the ground at speed.

The Osgur's team were also having a kickabout, and Eoin recognised Shane Pedlow, who he had played alongside for Leinster a couple of years before. Shane raised his hand in salute, which Eoin returned.

As soon as the players had completed their warm-up drills, Mr Carey signalled to them to return to the dressing room for the final preparations.

Inside, they stayed mostly silent, although the front-row players were whooping and hollering, banging their chests off each other like gorillas. The referee poked his head in the door, the signal that it was time to enter the arena.

CHAPTER 23

Eoin was glad that he got to take the kick-off, always preferring to have an early feel of the ball and a chance to kick it. He booted the ball high towards the stand side and jogged towards where it was about to land.

Both sets of forwards converged on the ball, and there was a roar from the stand as the players collided with each other. Rory Finnegan gathered the ball and the players formed a ruck around him before Mikey Conroy picked the ball off the ground and ducked around the short-side. With St Osgur's failing to cover, it was a master move and Mikey raced all the way to the corner where he dived to score.

'That must be the fastest try in the history of this place,' Rory shouted as the Castlerock players raced to congratulate Mikey.

'Great kick, Eoin,' said the try-scorer. 'Now go on and

make it seven.'

Eoin grinned as Mikey tossed him the ball and he collected the kicking tee from the ball-boy.

'Go on Madden,' roared Dylan, who was seated in the stand right on the 22. 'Let's get this over by half-time.'

Eoin smiled and teed up the ball. He went through his usual routine of stepping backwards, pausing, looking up at the posts, and running forwards while keeping his eyes on the ball. He kicked it straight and true, and despite it being a tricky kick from out wide, the ball went over the bar just inside the left-hand post.

St Osgur's were reeling from such an early blow and took several minutes to regain their composure, by which time they had conceded two more penalties, the second of which Eoin kicked to extend the lead to 10-0.

But St Osgur's did rally, and although Castlerock stayed on top for most of the first half, they were stunned just before the break. From a ruck in the Osgur's 22, scrum-half Cillian delayed just a half-second too long to pass to Eoin, and his arm was jogged, sending the ball high and wide of the out-half. Eoin reached to grab the ball, but his own pass to the inside centre was just as wayward. Shane Pedlow rushed into the gap and snatched the ball out of the air and set off on a run.

He dodged past the Castlerock full-back and as Eoin

remembered how speedy Shane was from the youth interpros he knew instantly there was no way he could be stopped.

Shane touched down under the posts and the teams went into the break with the score on 10-7, which was no reflection of how much Castlerock had bossed the first half.

'That was stupid,' snapped Eoin as he sat down in the dressing room at half-time. 'I should never have risked that pass.'

'Put it out of your head,' said Mr Carey. 'It's gone, ancient history. We need you to focus on the next forty minutes and what you do next if you get bad ball.'

Eoin nodded, and apologised for his outburst.

'Just keep doing what you're doing, men,' Mr Carey told the team. 'We're bossing them up front and that sort of pressure always leads to tries. Just stay disciplined – and don't give away any stupid penalties.'

CHAPTER 24

astlerock started the second half as they had started the first and were soon camped on the St Osgur's line. Their opponents' defence was better organised this time, however, and Castlerock struggled to find a way through. After seven or eight phases, an Osgur's player was penalised for entering the ruck from the side and Eoin took the opportunity to extend his team's lead to 13-7.

Eoin noticed that the tackles on him were becoming more frequent – and harder – and reckoned St Osgur's must have decided at half-time to target him.

But that just made him more determined to stay in the game and his natural speed and movement ensured he did not get into too much trouble. St Osgur's grew frustrated as Castlerock's solid defence held and with Eoin kicking another two penalties the game looked settled.

Alan and Dylan were at the front of the stand. 'It's all over now,' said Dylan, 'they won't come back from that.'

Alan frowned. 'A twelve- or thirteen-point lead is the most dangerous lead in rugby,' he told him. 'If they snatch a flukey try they are only five points behind. And all they need is another one and we're goosed. We need to keep the pressure on.'

Eoin was already doing the same calculation in his head and was in no mood to relax as he shouted support to his team-mates.

'Come on Castlerock,' he called as they took their places for the next line-out. 'No let up, let's keep the pressure up.'

Alan grinned at Dylan. 'He must have heard what I said.'

But try as St Osgur's might, they just couldn't find any gaps in Castlerock's defence and, once Eoin slotted another penalty to make it 22-7, they visibly wilted.

When the referee blew the final whistle, Eoin punched the air before shaking hands with the St Osgur's boys. 'Good luck in the final,' Shane Pedlow told him, 'it would be great if you were to win it.'

Eoin thanked him and wandered off to talk to his pals.

'You were great,' Alan told him. 'You'll be a definite starter for the final even if Johnny is back.'

Eoin winced. 'Steady on, Al, let's take it one game at a time – and enjoy winning this one!'

He returned to the dressing room where Mr Carey wore a very large grin. 'That was a cracking display, chaps,' he told them. 'We've a few things to work on but the control you showed in the second half was brilliant. Now we've three weeks before the final and let's all work hard at getting ourselves – and a winning plan – into shape by then. Most of you wouldn't have played at the Aviva before but I'm sure the others will fill you in on it.

'Sure, isn't it Eoin Madden's second home?' he added with a chuckle.

CHAPTER 25

Back at Castlerock Eoin found he had to walk really quickly to get up to his room without anyone stopping him to tell him how great he was.

'Thank you,' he would call over his shoulder as he raced along the corridors and up the staircases. He had to sidestep a couple of First Years who were looking for him to sign their match programmes.

'I'm sorry, I promise I'll sign later,' he told them politely.

When he reached the dormitory, he closed the door, laid his back against it and exhaled.

'Phew,' he told Alan and Dylan, who were lying on their beds reading. 'It's tough work being a celebrity.'

'Don't go looking for sympathy here,' said Dylan. 'No one's asked for my autograph since my match-winning performance at Dalymount Park.'

'Match-winning?' asked Alan. 'You didn't want to

bring on our real match-winner for the penalties, which was MY idea...'

'Now, now, lads,' said Eoin, 'It was a team game, so there were no "match winners" we all did our bit – including you, Alan.'

'Yeah we surely did,' said Alan. 'Is it really bad out there?' he asked, pointing at the door.

'Well it's not *bad*,' said Eoin. 'There's a lot worse things than being asked for your autograph all the time, but it does get a bit wearing after a while.'

'And with twenty-one more sleeps to the final it will only get worse,' said Alan. 'Can you imagine what it's going to be like as we get nearer to Castlerock's first senior cup final since we were all in nappies?'

'It could have a few nice privileges though,' suggested Dylan. 'There'll be no homework for you, and lots of second helpings at dinner, maybe extra chips.'

'Well first of all we're in Transition Year, so we don't have real homework anyway' replied Eoin. 'And I don't think we'd have much chance in the final if we were tucking into extra chips every night.

'It's just going to be rugby, rugby, rugby for the next three weeks, I don't expect I'll have much time for anything else except sleeping,' he added.

Eoin was right of course, as Castlerock went into full cup final mania. The school magazine announced it was bringing out a special edition and would be interviewing every member of the squad. Eoin hated being in the spotlight and hoped they might miss him out, but the editor stopped him after training one night.

'Hi, Eoin, can we arrange to meet you after school tomorrow in the 5A classroom?' he asked. 'We just need about half an hour, and a few photos too. Is that OK?'

Eoin shrugged and agreed to meet the reporter. 'I'm not very interesting,' he warned him.

★ ★ ★

He spent the next twenty-four hours in a bad mood, unhappy at the unwanted fuss about the final. He steered clear of the playground and common room where he knew he would be mobbed by first-year well-wishers. He decided to spend lunchtime down at The Rock and Alan asked could he join him.

'Yeah, no problem, let's jog down so we don't have to stop if anyone looks for my autograph,' Eoin grumbled.

Down in the hidden clearing Eoin jumped up and sat

108

on The Rock while Alan watched as a tiny fish darted between the pebbles on the bed of the stream.

'What should I say to this lad?' Eoin asked his friend.

'He'll have the questions,' replied Alan. 'All you have to do is reply to them. It will all straightforward stuff like your favourite film or what you eat before a match. He might ask you about New Zealand, or the match you remember best, but I wouldn't lose any sleep about it.'

Eoin shrugged his shoulders. 'I don't know, I have a bad feeling about this. What if he asks me about the ghosts?'

'How would he have heard about that?' said Alan. 'Only me and Dylan know your secret.'

'And what about Ross Finnegan?' asked Eoin. 'He met George Stack that time up in the dorm.'

'I don't think Ross would be running to the papers telling your secrets,' replied Alan. 'And I think he thought he'd dreamed it anyway?'

'But he wouldn't have to,' said Eoin. 'If he just let it slip to one lad, who let it slip to another, soon enough it would be all round the school.'

'And no one else has said a word to you,' said Alan. 'Which proves my point – you would have heard back by now if Ross had spilt the beans.'

CHAPTER 26

As soon as school ended Eoin headed up to the Fifth Year corridor and found room 5A. The reporter and photographer were waiting for him and introduced themselves as Theo and Benjy.

'I'll take a few shots of you here,' said Benjy, 'and maybe one or two at training tonight, if that's OK.'

Eoin struggled to work up a smile as he posed for a couple of photos.

'Right, so let's get down to the interview,' suggested Theo, directing him towards a desk.

Eoin sat down and Theo switched on a voice recorder app on his phone.

'When did you start playing rugby, Eoin?' he started.

Eoin thought back to his very first training session in the school and the embarrassment he felt when he made a mistake, thinking he was playing Gaelic football back in Ormondstown.

'Well, it wasn't very far from here,' he replied with a grin. 'Just outside this window! I'd never played rugby before I came to Castlerock, so I suppose Mr Carey was the one who taught me the game. Along with Mr Finn's coaching book,' he added, remembering the manual his grandad had given him, written by his old friend who had been a teacher at Castlerock.

'And you won a trophy in First Year,' Theo went on.

Eoin told the reporter the story of that successful campaign, and the ones that followed. Theo asked him about his selection for Leinster, and Ireland, and the British and Irish Lion Cubs tour to New Zealand. He quizzed him about the day he discovered the Aviva Stadium was in danger of collapse and his successful transfer to soccer during the previous term.

'And how have you settled into senior rugby this season?' he asked.

'I'm playing in a strong team, so they've helped make it as easy as possible for me,' Eoin replied, carefully. 'It's definitely a step up from the JCT, but I'm enjoying it and it's great to have the same coach as I had back in First Year again.'

Theo checked the phone was still recording before he turned back to Eoin.

'I just have one more question,' he told him, smiling. 'I hear talk that you've been talking to the ghost of a rugby player. What is that about? Does he visit you often?' he asked, grinning.

Eoin's face went bright red. 'Eh… no… are you joking? Where did you hear that?' he asked.

'I can't reveal my source,' replied Theo, 'but I understand you have been talking to a ghost in your dorm room.'

Eoin shook his head. 'I don't want to talk about that,' he said. 'I think your source could be mistaken.'

'Well did you, or didn't you? It's a yes or no answer,' pressed Theo, his eyes lit up.

Eoin was terrified about what to say. He couldn't risk adults finding out about Brian and George, and all the attention that would bring. He decided he couldn't tell the whole truth.

'I really can't tell you,' explained Eoin. 'It's a complicated story and no matter what I say people will think I'm crazy. Please don't write about this, please.'

Theo sighed. 'But Eoin, this is a really interesting story. People will want to read about it. It could even get on the television.'

'And that's exactly what I don't want,' Eoin snapped. 'I've enough on my plate with school and rugby without this coming along to mess my life up even more.

If you want to derail the senior cup team's bid for the first trophy in ten years then go ahead – I'm sure that will make you incredibly popular with everyone in the school!'

Theo frowned. 'That's not fair. I'm just interested in hearing about this ghost. I don't want to cause trouble.'

Eoin looked Theo straight in the eye. 'Listen, this is not something I asked for, or sought out. And I really don't want to talk about ghosts. Let me concentrate on the Senior Cup and maybe we can talk about it then.'

CHAPTER 27

Eoin was rattled by Theo's questions about George and stormed up the stairs to the dorm, ignoring all the autograph hunters and selfie seekers he met on the way.

He flung his schoolbag on the bed and let out an angry scream.

'What's up, Eoin?' asked Dylan. 'Didn't the interview go well?'

Alan stood up from his desk and walked over to his pal.

'Did he ask you about the ghosts?' he asked, and Eoin nodded.

'Yeah, Ross must have let it slip,' he sighed.

'Is he going to write about it?' asked Alan.

'I don't know,' Eoin replied. 'I told him it would ruin our chances of winning the cup so he might hold off until after the final. It's so annoying – I didn't want to explain it all to him, but any explanation is just going to make me sound bonkers.'

'I wonder is it worth…' Dylan's question was interrupted by a knock on the door. Ross Finnegan popped his head into the room and asked could he come in.

'Theo just called down to my room and said you were a bit upset,' he said. 'Was it something about the interview?'

Eoin nodded. 'Yeah, someone told him I was talking to ghosts. Any idea who that might have been?'

Ross hung his head.

'I'm sorry Eoin, I should have checked with you first. It's just that Theo is my twin brother – we don't look alike, I know – and he asked me to brief him on everyone in the team last week. I just came out with a few lines on all the guys… favourite band, strengths and weaknesses and all that. I had just been talking to you and mentioned that you had a ghost in your room. I suppose that does sound a bit stupid.'

Eoin paused. 'Oh well, that's not too bad. But can you get him to leave any mention of ghosts out of the article?'

Ross nodded. 'I'll tell him no one else will talk to him if he mentions anything about it. He's a good lad, he won't want to disrupt the campaign for the cup. I'm really sorry this happened, Eoin.'

Eoin smiled. 'No bother, Ross, if nothing appears in print it's fine. I'll explain the whole thing to you when we win the cup.'

There was no training the next afternoon, so Eoin ran down to the DART station and bought a ticket to Lansdowne Road. He enjoyed the short trip that whizzed past Dublin Bay before making its way through suburbia to the station beside the stadium.

He walked to the works entrance and asked for Simon in the Museum. Simon vouched for Eoin and so, with a yellow hard hat on his head and a plastic badge on a ribbon around his neck, he entered the stadium. He decided to take a longer route to the Museum, climbing the steps up onto the middle level and up into the grandstand. He looked down on the pitch where he had played some important games, and examined the far-left corner where he had spotted the structural problem that had caused the stadium to be closed for almost a year. It looked like most of the work had been done, and he hoped he would be able to get back there again as a spectator before too long.

He made his way down the staircase, checking if Brian was anywhere to be seen, and crossed to where the new Museum was taking shape.

'Hi, Simon, the place is really coming together, isn't it?' said Eoin as the curator came out to greet him.

'Well yes, we've done a lot of work since you were last here, and we've made a big show of the George Stack Collection, as you can see,' he replied, pointing towards a large display case in the centre of the room.

In the case was George's Ireland jersey being modelled on a mannequin, with his cap on the dummy's head. A printed board told the story of George and his career, and several of his letters and membership cards were also on display beneath a large photo of Ireland's first captain.

'That looks brilliant, I'm sure George will love it... I mean, I'm sure he would have loved to see it. Is the case locked and secure?' he asked.

'Well, yes,' replied Simon, 'But why do you ask? We take great care of the priceless artefacts people have lent or given us.'

'That's good to know,' said Eoin, glancing around to see who else was in the room with them. He lowered his voice and confided in the curator. 'It's just a friend of mine was passing by here last week and saw someone pocketing a gold medal…'

'Really?' said Simon. 'We had a very nice example of a Bateman Cup medal from the 1920s here recently, but no one can seem to find it now. Did your friend happen to see who took it?'

'He didn't know the man,' replied Eoin, 'but he said he was a small, slight chap with curly hair.'

Simon's eyes widened. 'That sounds familiar,' he muttered. 'I'll have to keep an eye on him.'

CHAPTER 28

Eoin kept a low profile for the rest of the week, spending his spare time at rugby training or hanging out with his pals in the dorm. The Rock also became a daily refuge from the cup-final mania that had taken hold in Castlerock.

The news from training was that Johnny Costello was back, at least in so far as he was able to jog laps around the pitch while the rest worked on plans to defeat St Malachy's.

'I don't think I'll be fit to play the final' he admitted to Eoin as they walked back to the dressing room. 'But Mr Carey's keen that I tog out so I expect they'll put me on the bench in case of emergencies. I expect that means you'll be the starting 10.'

Eoin nodded, not sure whether to commiserate with the senior boy or not. Instead he replied, 'I hope I'm able to fill your boots, Johnny, but it will be great if we could win you a senior medal.'

Johnny smiled. 'That would be nice, I never expected to win one of those so it would be a great bonus. But I really don't want to be wearing No.10 on my back in the Aviva – you've earned the shirt this term and you're our best hope to bring home the old silverware.'

Eoin changed his boots for a pair of runners and headed back towards his dorm for a shower before bed. As he climbed the stairs he bumped into his classmate, Sam Farrelly, who had given up rugby to join the school magazine team. Under his arm he was carrying a bundle of *The Castle Courier*.

'Hey, Eoin,' he started. 'Have you seen what we've written about you? The magazine is out tomorrow morning, but I can let you have a sneak preview,' he continued, as he handed him a copy.

Eoin thanked him, although not very warmly, and strode on towards the dorm. He stared at the front cover, which carried a photo of him in his Lion Cubs gear playing in a match in New Zealand.

'Castlerock's Cub' shouted the headline, with 'Youngest SCT out-half in history' printed underneath. Eoin sighed.

Back in the dorm Alan and Dylan were playing on their phones when Eoin arrived.

'Howya, hero,' called Dylan. 'Any news from training?'

'Looks like Johnny won't be starting anyway,' Eoin replied. 'You can probably read all about it in this,' added, tossing the school magazine onto his bed.

Alan hopped up and was just in time to snatch the publication before Dylan got there.

'Wow! You made the front page,' Alan said. 'You'll have to get that framed.'

Eoin grumbled, but said nothing in reply.

Alan flicked through the magazine till he found the pages about Eoin.

'I wonder will he mention the ghosts,' Dylan wondered aloud.

'I hope not,' replied Eoin. 'He's Ross Finnegan's brother and Ross said he'd square it with him.'

Eoin watched as Alan's eyes darted from line to line.

'It's great stuff,' he said, 'lots of big words praising you for all the trophies you won for Castlerock.'

He raced through the article and looked up at Eoin.

'You dodged that bullet,' he grinned. 'No mentioned of George Stack anyway. But there's something a bit funny about the article.'

Eoin frowned. 'What do you mean?' he asked.

'Well, some of the phrases he uses are a bit weird. It's like he's trying to tell you he knows something, but can't say it out loud.'

'Like what?' asked Eoin, puzzled.

'OK, how about this,' Alan started. '"Madden instilled a fighting *spirit* in his Ireland team-mates to help avoid the *spectre* of defeat," or "Madden's breaks *spooked* the New Zealand defence", or "He ran at the St Osgur's defence, *ghosting* past two players on his way to a memorable try".'

Dylan laughed. 'So he sneaked in four different words for ghost because he knew he couldn't write about the real ghost. That's gas.'

Eoin smiled and shrugged his shoulders. 'Oh well, at least he didn't leave me hanging out to dry. And no one could possibly guess what the private joke was from those words.'

CHAPTER 29

The magazine was all around the school next morning, ensuring Eoin got plenty of attention in the corridors and play areas of Castlerock. He was asked to sign about a dozen copies and was pestered by lots of boys wanting to know more about the things he'd discussed in the piece.

Even the teachers commented on it. 'Well Mr Madden, I'm glad to see your talents being lauded in print,' said Mr McGrath, who taught English. 'I hope that commitment to hard work will be seen next year when you get around to *tackling* Shakespeare.'

Eoin returned a thin smile while the rest of the boys cackled at the lame wisecrack.

'I will of course, sir,' he replied, before keeping his head down for the rest of the lesson.

He decided to go for a long run during lunch break, mainly to avoid any more unwanted attention. He changed into his tracksuit and slipped down the back stairs from the dorms to the rugby pitches. He counted out ten laps before heading off on a full circuit of the school grounds. As always, he ended his run by ducking into the bushes that hid The Rock.

As he caught his breath, he leaned back against the boulder and whispered, 'Are you around, Brian?'

'Can't you just wait for me to appear?' chuckled the ghost, as he moved into view.

'Sorry, Brian,' Eoin replied. 'I just needed to get away from the school and all the fuss about the final.'

'Why?' asked Brian.

'Well, it's just a bit irritating that the younger boys keep asking me for my autograph and to take a picture with me. I'd prefer to keep a low profile until it's all over.'

'Well, I don't know about that,' replied Brian. 'You're an important member of the school team about to play a very important match. These kids treat you as a hero because Castlerock is the centre of their world and the thought of the school winning the Senior Cup is an enormous thing to them, maybe even more than it is to you.

'They want to feel a part of it, and they love being able to connect with someone like you who is at the heart of the team. It's a small irritation for you to sign a piece of paper, or stand for a photo – maybe five or ten seconds? Even if you do a hundred of them it's still less than fifteen minutes out of your day – and you'd make a lot of youngsters very happy,' he added.

'So you think I should sign all the autographs?' asked Eoin.

'Well, yes,' replied Brian. 'And if you were to do them all at once you would be left alone. Try it.'

Eoin thanked Brian for his advice and walked slowly back towards the school. As soon as he entered, a First-Year boy asked him to sign his magazine.

'Yeah, of course,' said Eoin. He scribbled his name on the front page before he paused.

'Can you do me a favour?' he asked the youngster. 'Can you get the word around the First and Second Years that I'll be in the hallway outside the headmaster's office at four o'clock today. I'll sign everyone's magazine or whatever they want – and maybe then you'll all give me a break until after the final?'

The younger boy agreed and scurried off to tell his pals.

CHAPTER 30

After his autograph session, Eoin was able to enjoy a lot more peace in the run-up to the big game. There were still one or two requests every day, but he actually started to enjoy them; he liked talking to the younger boys and encouraging them to keep playing.

On his way to class one morning he called by the principal's office to check if any post had arrived for him. He never got much, except the odd card around birthday time, but that was still a few weeks away. So he was a little surprised when he found a stiff white envelope in the cubby hole.

'I wonder what this is?' he said to himself as he examined it. He slipped his fingernail under the flap and gently prised the envelope open. Inside was a piece of card that he took out and read. The card was mostly printed, but his own name was written in blue ink.

The President of the Irish Rugby Football Union
Has great pleasure in inviting
Mr Eoin Madden
to the opening ceremony for the new Irish Rugby Museum
at Aviva Stadium, Lansdowne Road
on Tuesday, March 17th at 12 noon.
RSVP

Eoin was at first stunned to receive the invitation, but when he thought a little more he was excited at the prospect of seeing the new museum.

When he got to his first class of the day he showed Alan the card.

'Wow, that's very cool,' his friend said. 'But will you be able to go?'

'Why not?' asked Eoin.

'Did you not see the date – it's on the same day as the Senior Cup final. The match kicks off at three o'clock, but I'm sure Mr Carey won't be very keen on you ducking off before the big game. They have that tradition of going for a walk on the beach and having lunch together. You'll struggle to escape for noon.'

'Oh no, you're right,' agreed Eoin. 'I doubt he'll let me off – but no harm in asking.'

During the next break in classes Eoin went looking

for the senior rugby coach. He found him talking to the headmaster outside the staff room.

'Ah, Mr Madden,' said the head, 'I do hope you're training hard for the big fixture. We're all extremely excited about the prospect of a cup win for Castlerock.'

Eoin smiled. 'Thank you, sir. I actually came to ask Mr Carey something about game day,' he said, handing the coach the invitation.

Mr Carey read the card and winced.

'Well now, that's a great honour for you, Eoin, and I presume you would love to attend,' said the coach, passing the invitation to the headmaster. 'But you know we have very important cup final day traditions here in Castlerock and very little time is your own on the day. After our stroll on the beach and Mr McCaffrey's speech, we will take a coach to Ballsbridge for an early light lunch in a hotel near the stadium. At 12.30pm we will walk the short distance to the ground to begin our preparations for the game. I really don't see how you could attend this event.'

'I'm afraid Mr Carey is right,' chipped in the headmaster. 'Although it's a great pity – your attendance would have been another feather in the cap of the school.'

'Perhaps I could leave lunch a little early and...' started Eoin.

'No, I don't think you should be breaking away from the group at that stage,' interrupted Mr Carey. 'You'll just have to send your apologies and say you cannot attend. I'm sorry.'

CHAPTER 31

Eoin thanked the two men, but inside he was annoyed. He would love to go to the opening ceremony and wasn't convinced that it would interfere in any way with the Senior Cup team's preparations for the game against St Malachy's.

'It's so unfair,' he told Alan when they got back to the dorm, but his friend did not reply.

'Do you not think I could have just jogged down from the lunch and had ten minutes at the Museum?' he asked.

Alan sighed. 'Yes, maybe,' he said. 'But you have to look at it from their point of view. Mr McCaffrey is obsessed with winning this cup, and there's huge pressure on Mr Carey to deliver it this year. He just doesn't want anything getting in the way of his goal, and he's afraid that his star player might get distracted – which you have a track record of around that stadium, to be fair!'

Eoin smiled at that. 'I suppose so,' he said, 'but what

could possibly go wrong at a Museum opening?'

'Maybe Simon would let *me* go instead?' suggested Alan. 'I know I didn't donate George's stuff, but I could, eh, sort of *represent* you there.'

Eoin laughed. 'That's very kind of you,' he replied sarcastically. 'I'm going to head into the Museum after school, so you could ask him yourself if you fancy tagging along?'

As soon as their last class was over the pair raced to the nearby DART station and bought two return tickets for Lansdowne Road.

'Just think,' said Alan. 'In ten days time there will be thousands of people on this train making this same journey just to cheer you on. All they will be talking about is you.'

Eoin looked out the window as the suburbs flew by. He had tried not to think too much about the final. And although he had played in several games with much bigger attendances, none was as important as this one to the people who were important to him. He really hoped he could live up to the faith they placed in him.

'Here we are so,' he said as the train slowed on the approach to the station. He pressed the button to open the carriage and stepped out on to the platform.

CHAPTER 32

Eoin and Alan collected their badges at the entrance gate, but were told they didn't need to wear hard hats anymore. The boys gazed up at the changes that had been made to the stadium in the months since their Christmas shopping outing.

'All the building work is done,' the security guard explained. 'It won't be long till the stadium reopens.'

'It's looks ready,' said Eoin as he clipped on his identity tag.

They walked briskly around to the Museum, which was close to completion. Eoin poked his head through the doorway in search of Simon, who was nowhere to be seen.

'Can I help you, boys?' came a voice from across the room.

'We were looking for Simon,' said Eoin as he and Alan moved inside.

'He's just stepped out for a few minutes; can I help you? I'm Steve, I'm Simon's assistant,' said the man, who Eoin recognised from George Stack's description.

'He's got curly hair,' said Alan under his breath.

'I had noticed that,' whispered Eoin to his friend.

'No, we'll wait for Simon if that's OK,' said Alan. 'Do you mind if we have a look around?'

'Fire away,' said Steve. 'But just make sure you don't touch anything,' he added before heading towards the offices at the back of the room.

'"*Don't touch anything*" – he's got some nerve,' said Eoin, once the assistant was gone from earshot.

The boys wandered around the room, marvelling at the amazing collection of jerseys, caps and programmes from some of Ireland's greatest victories down the years.

'I don't see anything from Ireland's first junior Four Nations win,' teased Alan, trying to get a reaction from his companion who was a key member of that team.

'I suppose that team wasn't too important really,' replied Eoin as he wandered around. 'But I see they've finished off the George Stack display.'

The mannequin wearing George's jersey and cap dominated the middle of the room.

'Wow,' said Alan. 'That looks very impressive, doesn't it? And there's all the other bits and pieces you gave him.

I wonder what George will think when he sees it?'

'I would say George would think it was quite a marvellous display,' came a voice from behind the boys.

'George!' said Eoin. 'You need to work on your entrances. You gave us all quite a fright there.'

'I do apologise' chuckled the ghost. 'What do you think of this tribute to my rugby career?'

'It's very nice,' said Alan. 'But it's a pity there's no really good photograph of you that survived.'

'Well, I didn't have my photo taken very often,' George answered. 'Maybe four or five times in my whole lifetime. Cameras were rare in those days, while nowadays it seems almost everyone has one in their pocket.'

'Maybe we could get Dylan to draw George – he's a really good artist.'

'That's a good idea, Al, we'll ask him tonight when we get back to school.'

'And how are preparations going for your Schools Cup Final?' asked George.

'All going well,' replied Eoin. 'The first-choice out-half is coming back from injury, but I think I'll be starting against St Malachy's.'

'And do you expect to win this game?' asked George.

'Well, I haven't played against them in Senior, but the guys on the team all say it's about fifty-fifty,' said Eoin.

'I must make sure I come along to watch the final,' said George.

'Well, it's on the same day as this place opens,' Eoin replied. 'Maybe you could come along for the opening ceremony too.'

'Which reminds me, we need to track down Simon,' said Alan.

Eoin pointed towards the back of the museum where Steve was visible behind the glass walls of his office.

'Is that the man you saw pocketing the medal?' he asked the ghost.

'He is the very one, indeed, the rogue,' George replied.

'We told his boss about him,' Eoin said. 'He said he'd keep an eye on him. He mustn't have enough proof yet.'

Another man entered the glass-windowed office.

'That's Simon, the boss,' said Alan. 'We actually came here to talk to him.'

When Simon looked up he spotted the boys and came out to greet them.

'Hello, Eoin, and Alan,' he said. 'Can you see how it's all coming together? Did you get the invitation to the opening?

'Well, that's what I came to ask you about,' said Eoin. 'Unfortunately, the opening is on the day of the Schools Senior Cup final over in the stadium – so I won't be able to attend.'

'Oh, that's a great pity,' said Simon. 'I was going to especially thank you in my speech – your donation is one of the centrepieces of the whole museum.'

'That's nice,' replied Eoin. 'It's just that I was wondering whether Alan could take my place at the ceremony? And maybe you could find room for my grandfather, who discovered all the George Stack treasures?'

Simon smiled and looked at Alan. 'Yes, of course,' he started. 'And Alan would be more than welcome too. I hope it's not too boring for you, but we will have sausage rolls.'

Alan grinned. 'Oh well, count me in so, thanks very much,' he said.

CHAPTER 33

Eoin's days settled into a very steady pattern of sleep-eat-train-class-train-eat-sleep. Even the classwork was very untaxing as they neared the end of term. There was a project to work on for business studies, but he was letting Alan make all the running on that.

Training was getting more intensive, however and they also had a few Castlerock old boys in to talk to them about what it meant to win the Schools Senior Cup when they were at the school. One of the men, Ollie, went on to play for Ireland and the Lions and was one of the photographs on the wall in the school's hall of fame.

'I played in front of 50,000 people in Lansdowne Road, 80,000 in Twickenham, and 90,000 in Sydney,' he told the boys. 'But I tell you one thing with my hand on heart – nothing was more exciting, or more daunting, than putting this jersey on and walking out at Lansdowne Road on Schools Cup final day. It chilled me to the bone, I was really terrified that I would let people down, especially our coach Mr Andy Finn. But he told us something that day that I remembered throughout my whole career – 'the team that makes the fewest mistakes will win.'

'It's a simple phrase, but it's so true. Rugby games are lost by mistakes – wayward passes, silly offsides, missed tackles. If you each focus on your job and cut out the mistakes, I'm sure you'll win the game. And trust each other – the player beside you won't make mistakes either. So focus on your job – don't go chasing other people's jobs because you don't trust them to do it themselves. Remember – if you set off to chase two rabbits you will never catch any, but if you set off to chase one, well that's a much easier proposition. And if you focus on the task in hand you WILL win the Senior Cup. And after all I achieved in rugby it is still the single victory I value the most.'

After training the boys and Ollie were invited into the hall for a cup of tea and sandwiches where Eoin got talking to the former pupil.

'Was Mr Finn a good coach?' Eoin asked him. Andy Finn was a great friend of Dixie Madden since they had been at school in Castlerock together more than half a century before.

'He was indeed,' replied Ollie. 'He taught me more about rugby than any other coach. He had such a great ability to get the message across to boys. Nowadays he would be coaching Leinster or Munster, no doubt, but there was no money in rugby in those days. And anyway, wasn't he a brilliant teacher too!'

Eoin nodded in agreement.

'Andy has retired a good few years now, how did you know him?' asked Ollie.

Eoin explained how his grandfather and Andy were pals.

'And did your grandad play or coach?' asked Ollie.

'Well, he played a good bit, but never coached as far as I know,' Eoin replied. 'His name is Dixie Madden.'

Ollie's eyes widened. 'Wow, the famous Dixie. We heard all about him from Mr Finn. He was supposed to have been a seriously good player, but there was no video footage of him available, so I never saw him play.'

'He gave me a copy of Mr Finn's book,' Eoin replied. 'It's really good and helped me a lot when I was still learning the game.'

'Ah yes, I remember getting that for Christmas when I was about ten,' said Ollie, with a smile. 'And I think I remember that Dixie came to talk to our Senior Cup team before the final. It's funny how history goes around in circles, isn't it.'

Ollie moved to talk to another group of boys and Eoin went to ask Johnny how he was getting on.

'I'm almost back to full training, Eoin,' he said. 'But I don't think I'll be up to a full game. They usually go for a 60-20 split in terms of minutes, but I think you'll be the one they start with. You deserve it!'

CHAPTER 34

The following night was the last training session before the final, and every member of the squad was there early, not wanting to give the coach any excuse to drop him. Eoin lifted his kitbag onto the bench and started to change into his tracksuit.

The coach arrived soon after.

'Thanks for getting here early, guys,' said Mr Carey. 'We have a good idea what the team will look like for the final, but we want to run through a few things and check on the fitness of a couple of players. Nothing too physical tonight though, we don't want any more injury headaches ahead of the Aviva Stadium.'

The boys made their way out on to the training pitch, where there were more than a few spectators eager for a glimpse of their heroes before the big day.

After they went through the usual series of warm-up exercises, Mr Carey called them all together on the half-way line.

'Right so, we've split you all into two teams. I won't lie to you – the team who will be wearing the orange bibs is what we think should be our starting fifteen against St Malachy's. We're more interested in working through the moves and set-plays, so no rough stuff.'

He read the names out and to Eoin's relief his name was on the orange team. Miss Neville, one of the assistant coaches, handed him a bib.

Johnny Costello, wearing a green bib, winked across at Eoin as they took their places for the practice match.

It was almost dusk when they started the game, so the floodlights came on just as Eoin took the kick-off. Some of the boys on the green team were obviously disappointed not to be selected for the final, but when the first of them went in hard for a tackle Mr Carey whistled up and spoke to him sternly.

The game was very stop-start, with the coaches frequently halting play to explain something they wanted the players to improve upon. Eoin found it frustrating, as he really preferred when the game flowed quickly and he could create scoring chances for others. As the game neared the end he turned to one of those moves he like to execute. As the orange team surged forward he spotted Oisín had gone out from centre onto the wing, so

Eoin kicked the ball into the space between the 22 and try-line for him to chase.

Oisín was quick, but Johnny Costello was quick too and he raced across to cover. The orange team centre arrived at the ball a split second ahead of Johnny, but although Oisín gathered the ball cleanly his opponent was able to fling himself at him and bundle him roughly into touch.

Eoin heard Oisín's cry before he hit the ground.

'What did you do that for?' he groaned as he lay flat out.

A concerned Mr Carey rushed over to check on Oisín. 'Where does it hurt?' he asked.

'My ribs, sir,' he said. 'He came flying through the air and poleaxed me. I think I've cracked one!'

'Miss Neville, can you go find the nurse please?' asked Mr Carey, who turned with a stern face to Johnny Costello, who looked mortified.

'What did you do that for, Costello?' he thundered. 'Did you not hear me say we didn't want anyone being injured before the final. That tackle was reckless.'

'I'm sorry, sir,' said Johnny. 'I haven't played for so long and it was just instinct to try to stop him scoring. Sorry, Oisín…'

The school nurse arrived and checked him out and

said she didn't think he had broken anything, but he would need ice and painkillers. 'And no rugby for four weeks I'm afraid,' she added.

Oisín's face crumpled as he fought hard not to cry. Eoin even thought Mr Carey might join him.

CHAPTER 35

The session was abandoned, and the coach was too busy making sure Oisín was being looked after to give his usual end-of-training speech. The dressing room was quiet as the boys changed.

There was none of the usual banter walking back to the school either, just Ross talking quietly to Johnny, reassuring him that it was just a freak accident and no one blamed him for it. Eoin agreed, but still thought Johnny had been careless in unleashing a flying tackle like he had.

Back in the dorm Eoin filled in his pals on the events of the evening.

'So, who's going to take Oisín's place in the centre?' wondered Alan.

'It's a headache for Mr Carey, right enough,' replied Eoin. 'The game is in less than two days.'

'Louie Murphy is a direct replacement from the

second fifteen, but he's not that great, is he?' said Dylan.

Eoin shrugged. 'I suppose Mr Carey could play Johnny Costello there, but he'd struggle to play the full game.'

'It wouldn't look great either, letting him take advantage of the injury he caused,' said Alan.

'I wonder would he consider a nippy winger from last year's Junior Cup Team?' suggested Dylan.

Alan laughed. 'That's very kind of you to offer, Dyl, but I'd say they could come up with a better solution.'

'Well, I'm ready, willing and able,' Dylan said, picking up a pillow and passing it straight to Eoin. 'You tell him that.'

Eoin snorted, returned the pillow and tossed his kitbag in the corner.

'Go on, I've done a class drawing of George like Alan suggested,' said Dylan, showing his friend the sketch, which he admitted was very accurate.

'Thanks Dyl, that's class, but I'm going to sleep now and I don't want to be woken up by anything except the smell of sausages coming up from the kitchen at breakfast time,' he said before he lay down on his bed.

Next morning Eoin got up early for a run before

breakfast. After a couple of laps of the rugby pitches, he ducked into the bushes that surrounded The Rock. Brian was waiting there for him.

'Hello, Eoin, it won't be long till the big game then. Have you found out whether you're starting or not?' he asked.

Eoin took a deep breath before explaining the events of the night before.

Afterwards, Brian asked, 'And this guy Oisín, is he an important player?'

'Well, he's not a major star, but he's been on the team for a couple of years and knows all the moves. It will be hard to replace him,' replied Eoin.

'But does it mean you're more likely to start?' asked Brian.

Eoin shrugged. 'It really depends what Mr Carey is thinking. He still might decide to take a chance on Johnny. Or maybe even go back to Kieran Hickey. This just complicates things.'

'Your friend George has been around the stadium; I've run into him a couple of times. He's quite excited about the museum showing his old gear, but he keeps going on about stuff being stolen.'

'Yes, he saw one of the men who works there pocketing a medal – we pointed him out to Simon, who's in charge of the museum.'

'I must make sure to drop by the museum when they open it up, I'm sure I'd remember seeing many of the players in action there over the years. I won't need an invitation anyway,' he joked.

Eoin jogged back to the school where he met the postman arriving with a sack of letters.

'Do you want a hand with those?' he asked, and the grateful postman allowed him to carry the bag into the headmaster's office.

'Are there any letters for me, Eoin Madden?' he asked as the postie started to sort through the contents of his sack.

'I think so,' he replied, 'Give me a minute to sort them out.'

Eoin watched as he flicked through the envelopes and packets, eventually stopping and picking a small white envelope out of the bundle.

'Here you are,' the postman said, 'I remember your name – you're the lad that saved all those people in Lansdowne Road, aren't you?'

Eoin blushed, and mumbled his thanks.

Outside the head's office he sat on a bench and opened the envelope. He recognised the handwriting as that of his grandfather.

'Dear Eoin,' he read. 'I hope you're keeping well and working hard. And of course I hope you're fighting fit for this big game at the Viva. Your dad is driving me and your mam up, so we'll be there to cheer Castlerock on. I got an invitation to the opening of the Museum so I might see you there if you have time. I found a few more bits and pieces in that old house we were helping to clear – the Museum might be interested in some of them. I'm just a little concerned that they'd put me in one of their cabinets as I'm a bit of a rugby relic myself!'

Eoin laughed and returned the letter to the envelope, where he spotted his grandfather had enclosed a twenty euro note.

'Thanks, Grandad,' he whispered with a smile as he headed off to breakfast.

CHAPTER 36

Eoin spent the morning watching an old black and white movie in Film Studies class. Just as the film reached an important scene a knock came to the door and Ross poked his head around the door.

'Sorry, teacher,' he said. 'Mr Carey just asked me to tell Eoin Madden there would be a team meeting in the hall at lunchtime. Apologies for barging in.'

Eoin tried to concentrate on the rest of the movie, but Ross's interruption had brought him back to the real world and the murmurs and whispers from the rest of his class meant he totally missed the ending and what it meant.

'Do you think you're in the team?' asked Sam Farrelly as the class filed out of the room.

Eoin shrugged his shoulders. 'Who knows?' he replied. 'We're going to miss Oisín, but there are still a few options for the coach.'

'I've a brother in First Year who's your number one fan,' said Sam. 'He will be so gutted if you don't play. Bobby is always asking me to get your autograph.'

Eoin smiled thinly. 'OK, but maybe leave it till after the final, I've nothing to write on now.'

By the time lunchtime arrived Eoin was completely caught up with all the various ways Mr Carey might solve the problem. He rushed to the canteen to grab a chicken wrap before he made his way to the hall to join his team-mates.

The coach was standing with his back to the stage, with the players in a semi-circle around him.

'Good afternoon, Eoin,' he said. 'Join the group here and we'll start.'

Eoin slipped in beside Johnny Costello, who gave him a grin and a thumbs up.

What does he mean by that? wondered Eoin. *Did Mr Carey give him a sneak preview of the team?*

Eoin's mystery was solved pretty quickly.

'OK, guys,' the coach started. 'I was all set to tell you the team last night, but unfortunately Oisín's injury threw our plans up in the air. The good news is that he hasn't broken anything, but he's not going to play any more rugby this season.'

A murmur of sympathy rippled through the gathering. Eoin noticed that Johnny was staring at the floor.

'So… we had a number of options around the middle of the field, and recognising we might to make changes during the game, we have decided to start with Kieran at centre and Johnny at out-half. Young Eoin will be our game-changer, ready to come in anywhere we need to make an impact. We're confident that we have a winning combination here and can continue the great form that has got us into the final.'

Eoin was a little disappointed not to make the starting fifteen, but he knew he would be called upon to play a part in the game. Most of the team left the room chattering about the selection, but Mr Carey asked Eoin, Johnny and Kieran to wait.

'Right you three, it's unfortunate that we were forced into these changes, but we have done what we think is best for the team. You all know our plans and we expect everyone to put every effort in to winning this game for the school.

'Eoin, we expect you to remain focused on the sideline and to be ready to join the fray at any stage. Our usual procedure is to replace the half-backs with twenty minutes left, if necessary, but it may turn out that we need you to go on as early as half-time.'

Eoin nodded and listened as the coach took the other

two through their roles.

As they were leaving, Johnny tapped Eoin on the shoulder.

'Are you disappointed, Eoin?' he asked.

'I suppose I am, just a little,' Eoin replied. 'But you've been the main man on this team for years, I've only come in because you were injured. I've no right to expect to go straight into the team. But if you're not a hundred per cent I expect Mr Carey will bring me on.'

'Yeah, and that's fair enough,' replied Johnny. 'I do feel good and the injury has cleared up, but I haven't tested it in a big match yet. I'll know fairly quickly how I'm getting on.'

CHAPTER 37

The rest of the day was a bit of a blur for Eoin. Everyone he met, even boys he had never seen before, wished him luck in the final. He always hated the run-up to big games, when all he wanted was to be togged for action and walking out on to the field.

After dinner he asked Alan to come down to the rugby pitch to help him practise his goal-kicking. Eoin borrowed six balls from the dressing room and lined them up far out on the left around the 22.

'I want to practise my kicks out wide,' he told Alan. 'I'd be confident of nailing anything towards the middle, but these are much harder as the posts seem to get narrower.'

Alan took his place under the posts and signalled with his arm over his head every time Eoin successfully goaled. Eoin missed one from his first set of six, and one from the next one too, but he nailed all six of the third series of kicks and decided he was happy with that.

He moved across to the right-hand side of the field and propped the ball up on the tees.

'This is usually your weaker side,' said Alan, who kept lots of statistics on Eoin's kicking. 'If you can convert five out of six from here you'll be doing better than you've ever done before.'

Eoin missed the first three kicks, but as he found his range he found it easier to hit the target, banging over the next three. He took six more and converted five.

'Great work, Eoin,' called out Alan. 'Now let's give it a two more sets, I'm getting cold here.'

Eoin nodded and set out the six balls and took his kicks. Four went over cleanly, one off the inside of the post but the sixth was caught by the wind and pulled narrowly wide.

Eoin raged at the sky, demanding a re-kick, but Alan laughed at him.

'There'll be wind blowing at the Aviva too,' he reminded him. 'Now's your last chance for the grand prize.'

Eoin calmed down and set up the final six balls. He took a deep breath and began his run up. One, two, three, four, five all split the posts.

'Come on, Eoin, you can do it!' Alan called as he settled himself before the final kick. He tossed a few blades of grass in the air just to test whether the wind was going to intervene once again.

He took aim and kicked the ball straight and true between the posts before leaping and punching the air.

'Wahoo!' shouted Alan. 'That was a gem. I hope you get a chance to take a few kicks tomorrow now!'

Eoin helped Alan gather the balls and return them to the dressing room.

'Let's do two quick laps to help us sleep,' suggested Eoin.

'I'll have no problem sleeping,' laughed Alan. 'But then again I don't have anything to worry about tomorrow except missing the bus to the Aviva.'

But he joined his pal as they jogged around the field and down past the Rock before they finished up at the main door of the school.

'Good night, Mr Madden and Mr Handy,' said the headmaster who was standing outside. 'I hope you get plenty of sleep tonight.'

'Thank you, sir,' replied Eoin. 'That's what I was doing, getting some kicking practice in and a jog to tire me out.'

'Excellent thinking,' said Mr McCaffrey. 'I've just been talking to Mr Finn, who is planning to come along tomorrow. I've invited him to join us for lunch too.'

'That's great, sir,' said Eoin. 'My grandfather will be delighted to see him again.'

CHAPTER 38

Eoin's plan to tire himself out worked perfectly and he was only woken next morning by the sound of Alan's alarm clock.

'Gotta fly, guys,' he told his room-mates as he dressed quickly. 'We've a team breakfast, a team walk on the beach and a team lunch. My whole life is on a timetable today.'

'Good luck, mate,' said Dylan, 'we'll be watching from our usual spot so give us a wave when you get on.'

Eoin raced down the corridors, not because he was late, but so he didn't have to stop and talk to everyone who wished him luck in the final.

Castlerock, having been regular contenders for the Senior Cup over many years, had developed several traditions around the team on the day of the final. Even though it had been more than a decade since the school had been in the final the boys were well aware of all that would happen on the day.

The first of those traditions was to eat breakfast as a team, taking over the top table in the dining hall, with the teachers having to eat their breakfast elsewhere on this one day in the year. Eoin enjoyed sitting at the staff table again, which was a lot nicer than the ones he ate at every morning. The seats were much more comfortable and there were large jugs of orange juice and apple juice for refills instead of the single tiny glass the pupils were usually given.

The headmaster and the rugby coaches also sat at the table and the conversation up and down the line was all about the game ahead. Oisín, too, was invited to dine with the team and he sat beside Johnny – their friend-ship had clearly survived the reckless tackle.

After breakfast, the headmaster rose and said a few words to the school.

'Castlerockians,' he began. 'Today is a day that is highly prized in our school calendar, but one that has been all too rare in recent years. A very special group of pupils have battled their way through to the final of the Senior Cup and we should all be enormously proud of these young men. They deserve a round of applause for a start,' he added before starting to clap and encouraging every-one else to join in.

The head called them up one by one, including replacements, and the boys cheered and clapped every player. Eoin, being the sole Transition Year student, got an especially loud cheer, among which he could pick out Dylan roaring 'Go on Eoin, ye good thing ye!'

After breakfast, the boys collected their gear from their rooms and met up once again at the headmaster's office. Inside they were each presented with their game shirt, which had been specially embroidered with the line 'Senior Cup final – Castlerock College v St Malachy's School' with the date underneath. Eoin collected his and checked the shirt number – 23 – before he tucked it in his kit bag.

The next final day tradition was the walk on the beach near the school, and Mr Carey led them on a light jog out as far into Dublin Bay as they could reach before reaching the low tide coming in. Eoin turned back and faced the coastline, marvelling at the sweep of the city and its suburbs and admitting that he had grown to love the capital city.

'Any nerves at all?' Hugh, one of the props, asked Eoin as they walked back to the school.

'Are you joking,' interrupted Ross. 'This lad has played at Twickenham and the Cake Tin in Wellington. He's played in the Aviva more times than you've even watched a match there. Eoin has nerves of steel.'

Eoin tried hard not to blush and muttered how he always felt a little nervous before a big game.

'I hope you get a run,' said Hugh. 'We're lucky to have someone on the bench who could lift our game if we need it.'

Back at the school they relaxed and chatted to their friends for half an hour before a large luxury coach pulled into the school grounds.

'All aboard for the Aviva!' called Mr Carey as the boys lined up to board the bus.

Suddenly, hundreds of boys poured out of their class-rooms and lined up along the avenue to wave their heroes off. As the bus slowly moved past them Eoin looked out the window and waved whenever he saw a face he recognised. All those faces, all expecting nothing but success and glory this afternoon. Eoin really hoped they would not be disappointed.

CHAPTER 39

The bus left the boys at a hotel at the other end of Lansdowne Road, just a short walk from the stadium. An old man waiting at the entrance of the hotel waved to the boys as they walked towards him.

'Ah, Mr Finn, I just *knew* you'd be along today,' said Ross.

'Thank you for coming, Andy,' said Mr Carey, 'I understand Mr McCaffrey has invited you to join us for our early lunch.'

'Yes, he kindly asked me to come along. I've been at quite a lot of these pre-match lunches, but not for a very long time,' he replied.

The boys were shown into a small dining room where Mr McCaffrey was waiting for them. All around the walls he had hung photos of previous Castlerock teams that had won the Senior Cup.

'I hope we have a picture of you lads on the wall next

year – and that we're back here with Eoin Madden and his team,' he told them.

Eoin smiled, and took his seat alongside Johnny Costello.

'I don't think we get to order ourselves,' Johnny moaned. 'Mr Carey got some Leinster Rugby guy to give the hotel a menu for us. All chicken and pasta, I expect.'

Johnny was nearly right – there was a choice between a chicken salad and chicken and rice dish. Eoin chose the latter, but his appetite had gone missing and he barely picked away at it.

Mr Finn was sitting at the top of the table with the headmaster and Mr McCaffrey, and when he noticed Eoin had finished eating he beckoned to him to join them.

'I was just telling Mr McCaffrey about the new Museum in the stadium – Dixie filled me in on how you played a role in one of the exhibits.'

Eoin explained about the George Stack artefacts, found by Dixie, that he had brought to the museum.

'I'm going to the opening shortly,' said Mr Finn, 'I presume you will be coming along too?'

Eoin looked nervously at Mr Carey.

'Well… I do have a big match today, so it's probably

best if I stay with the team,' he replied.

'As you are not in the starting fifteen, surely Mr Carey can allow you to represent the school at this prestigious occasion,' said Mr Finn.

Mr McCaffrey smiled. 'I've been thinking about this Mr Carey, and I'm inclined to let Mr Madden attend this event. Mr Finn can accompany Eoin to ensure he does not get into any trouble, and he could even be back at the stadium before we arrive there.'

Mr Carey shrugged his shoulders. 'I suppose so,' he said. 'Just make sure you don't get distracted and find the goalposts are going to collapse or whatever. You're famous for that sort of thing.'

Eoin thanked the teachers. 'My gear?' he wondered, but Mr Carey assured him that everyone's kit had been brought to the stadium and would be waiting for them in the dressing room.

'Well, thank you very much headmaster,' said Mr Finn. 'I'll be delighted to chaperone this young man at the opening, and I will report to you about what they say about him and the school.'

Eoin and the retired teacher left the hotel and walked briskly down Lansdowne Road to the stadium chatting about all the previous days they had been there for a final. Mr Finn showed his invitation and explained that

Eoin had left his back in the school. The security guard grumbled about it, but recognised Eoin from his earlier visits and eventually let the pair of them in.

CHAPTER 40

Eoin showed Mr Finn the way to the Museum, and they joined another short queue to enter the building. Simon greeted them and said he was delighted that Eoin had been able to attend after all. Inside he saw Billy the engineer, Ollie the Castlerock old boy, and a few other familiar faces, mostly star players from the past among a large crowd of visitors.

'They let you come!' came a voice from behind him. 'That's brilliant – and yes, they *do* have really nice sausage rolls…'

'Alan!' said Eoin, as he turned around. 'I hope you're behaving yourself. Mr Finn has arrived to keep an eye on you.'

'I'm not keeping an eye on you two,' said the old teacher. 'I trust you know how to conduct yourselves at an event like this. Keep an eye on the clock Eoin, you're like Cinderella at the ball I'm afraid. You will have to be out of here in forty minutes – and I'm going to be busy chatting to my great friend who has just arrived,' he added, as he put out his hand to greet Dixie Madden.

'Grandad!' said Eoin, 'I forgot you were coming to this. I must show you the George Stack exhibits!' he exclaimed, before steering the group through the crowds towards the middle of the floor.

They all marvelled at the mannequin that was now adorned with George's cap and jersey, as well as a pair of long knickerbocker shorts that were the style in the 1870s. The boots were fearsome objects, and Eoin wondered what it would have been like to run in such heavy-looking footwear.

'Donated by Mr Richard Madden,' Eoin read from the inscription at the bottom of the card that explained who George was. On the other side of the exhibit a figure appeared wearing exactly the same clothing as the mannequin.

Eoin smiled at George who winked back at him.

'Gosh, I didn't think I would get my name in lights,' said Dixie. 'That's quite an honour.'

'Now don't be modest, Dixie,' said Mr Finn. 'You are fully worthy of a place in this pantheon of the greats.'

'Eh, what's a pantheon?' asked Alan.

'I'm sorry, it's Greek for "all the gods" – it's a place

where they believed all the great heroes would go. Dixie is one of the brightest stars in the pantheon of Castlerock College,' replied Mr Finn.

Dixie shook his head and laughed softly. 'Now, now Andy, you're being silly. Young Eoin here is a better player now than I was at his age. And that reminds me, I have a few more goodies for you, Eoin.'

He produced a large plastic carrier bag, which he handed to Eoin. 'There were a lot more items in the attic of that house. The owner was a bit of a collector. I don't know how useful these are, but there are a few nice medals and some old photos too.'

Eoin thanked his grandfather and said he would give them to Simon.

'There's some fantastic things in here,' said Alan once they found a quiet corner to check out the contents. Eoin reached into the bag and lifted out a small wooden box before opening it.

'Wow,' said Alan, taking a deep breath. 'They look like they're solid gold.' Eoin picked up one of the medals and read on the back 'Bateman Cup winners 1929, Lansdowne RFC'.

'That's Brian's old club,' said Eoin. 'I wonder is there any more stuff from them here.' He took out the rest of the medals and counted seven in all, including one with

'Schools Senior Cup 1924' engraved on it. He took a quick photo with his phone of the set of medals.

'There's Simon over there,' said Alan, 'let's show him what Dixie brought.'

The boys rushed over to where the curator was talking to some guests.

'Excuse me, Simon, sorry to interrupt, but could we have a quick word?' Eoin asked.

'Ah, Eoin, Alan, thank you very much for coming today. I'm afraid I'm very busy now and am just about to make a speech so I can't talk to you till afterwards.'

'But we have a new bag of medals and photographs Dixie would like to donate to the museum,' said Eoin.

'And we have a drawing of George that is very accurate, too,' added Alan.

'Well, that's very nice of you,' he replied. 'But I can't examine them now.'

He looked around the room. 'I can't see anyone else from our staff,' he said, before pausing. 'But wait, there's Steve, he'll be able to help you,' pointing towards the back of the room where his workmate was standing.

Eoin was reluctant at first, but he thanked Simon and the boys made their way to where Steve was standing.

'Do you think it's OK to give this stuff to him?' he asked Alan.

'I dunno, I suppose Simon must have checked him out if he's still working here,' Alan replied.

'Hi! Steve, isn't it?' Eoin started. 'Simon told me you might be able to help us. We have a bag of artefacts here we'd like to donate to the museum.'

Steve's eyes widened as Eoin showed him the bag, and he beckoned the boys to join him in the office.

'Are you enjoying the opening,' he asked them as he showed them inside. 'Your George Stack exhibit is proving to be very popular.'

'Thanks,' Eoin replied, noticing that George's ghost had followed them into the office.

'Now what have we got here?' Steve asked as he lifted the bag onto the counter and began to unload the contents.

CHAPTER 41

Steve put the photographs in a neat pile on one side of the desk and carefully opened the small wooden box.

'My, my aren't these little beauties?' he said as he lifted them on to the desk. He took a magnifying glass out of a drawer in the desk and began to examine the medals.

'I think they're from someone who played for Lansdowne,' said Eoin.

'Yes indeed,' said Steve. They date from the 1920s when Lansdowne were one of the strongest sides in the country. At one stage all four of the Irish three-quarters line were from the club – imagine.'

Steve wrote some notes on a sheet of paper and started to put the medals back in the box.

'Oh, look, Simon is about to start his speech,' he announced, pointing out the window towards the top of the room.

When Alan and Eoin turned back Steve was putting the magnifying glass back in the drawer, which he closed and locked.

He put the wooden box and the photos into a filing cabinet and locked that too. *That's reassuring*, thought Eoin. *They'll be safe in there.*

'We have to be very careful around here,' Steve said. 'Some of the items have gone missing since we started this project.'

As the trio went to leave the office George waved at Eoin to hang back.

'He only put five medals back in the box,' the ghost whispered. 'He must have stolen the others. I saw him do it with my own eyes.'

Eoin shook his head in annoyance. 'He's the one I told Simon about,' he told George. 'I can't *believe* he let him take the medals off us. I'll have to tell Simon.'

The museum curator was on a small stage at the top of the room, where he started to talk. 'We have such a valuable shared history here in this room, of rugby, of football and of several other sports that have been played on this sacred site. We have shirts, medals and playing equipment from the archery club, from cricket, lacrosse, tennis, rifle-shooting and cycling. The ground was built of course by an athletics club, so we have a large display on those early champions.

'But of course the stadium is full these days mainly for rugby and football, and I see some of the great players that played here have come along today. I met a gentleman who played rugby here in the 1940s and I met another youngster who will be playing here today in the Schools Senior Cup final. That player was also a kind donor, with his grandfather Dixie Madden, of the wonderful collection of items belonging to George Stack, the very first captain of the Irish rugby team. Many thanks to them both, and good luck to Eoin when he turns out for Castlerock here later this afternoon.'

The audience applauded and Mr Finn gave Eoin a thumbs up signal from across the room. Ollie came up behind him and patted him on the back.

Simon went on to welcome all the guests and suggested a few of the exhibits that they check out before they left. He was followed on the stage by a government minister and representatives of the two major sports that owned the stadium who all made short speeches.

Once the ceremony was over Eoin checked the time and realised he had just over ten minutes left before he would have to leave to join up with his team-mates.

'I'll have to tell Simon now,' he told Alan. 'Will you come along too?' Alan nodded and followed his friend as he made his way up to the stage.

Again Eoin interrupted the curator and asked could he have a private word. Simon looked a little annoyed, but agreed and pointed him towards the office at the back.

CHAPTER 42

'I'm sorry, Simon,' Eoin said once they were in the office with the door closed. 'Alan and I have just witnessed something very worrying – and annoying.'

Simon's eyebrows rose. 'What was that, boys?' he asked.

Eoin explained about the box full of medals, and how Steve had not returned them all to it. He pointed out the filing cabinet where the items had been locked inside.

Simon fished a bunch of keys from his pocket and opened the cabinet. He removed Eoin's bag and placed it on the desk just as Steve walked into the room.

'Ah, the boys are showing you their latest donation, are they?' he asked.

'Well yes, I suppose they are,' said Simon, carefully. 'Have you examined the contents?'

'Yes, we were in here before the speeches,' replied Steve. 'I made some notes about the medals – they're all from the 1920s and 1930s – three Leinster Senior

Cup, one Provincial Towns Cup and one other I wasn't able to identify. I didn't have a chance to examine the photographs.'

Simon carefully placed all the items on the desk.

'So, there were five medals in all then?' he asked.

Steve nodded, 'Yes, there are five in that box.'

Eoin suddenly remembered something and spoke up. 'I have a photo I took of the box just before we went to see you,' he said, taking his mobile out of his pocket. 'Here it is,' he added as he showed them the photo. 'Seven medals. The schools one is missing, and the Bateman Cup medal.'

Steve seemed shocked. 'I don't understand that,' he said. 'There were only five medals when I examined the box. I sincerely hope you are not accusing me of taking them.'

Simon frowned. 'No one is accusing you of anything,' he said. 'The boys say they brought seven medals in here and you say there were five. So how can we account for the other two?' he asked.

Eoin noticed that Brian had just appeared behind Simon and was pointing at something and making faces. Eoin tried to make out what he was trying to say. As only Alan and Eoin could see him, Brian just pushed past Simon and crouched down, pointing at the desk drawer. Eoin suddenly realised what he was trying to explain.

'They're in that drawer,' he said, pointing at where he now remembered Steve had put the magnifying glass. 'He put his magnifier back into it and locked it just before we left.'

Simon looked at Steve. 'Why would you lock your stationery drawer?' he asked. 'Would you mind opening it for me, just to clear this up?'

Steve started to get angry. 'Now hang on, you can't just believe a couple of kids who come in making accusations.'

'I'm not believing anyone,' said Simon. 'I'm the manager of this museum and I want to see what's inside one of the drawers in our offices. If you won't open it, I will ask the Garda outside to break it open.'

Steve went pale. He thought for a moment and handed over his bunch of keys. 'It's the small silver one,' he said.

Simon opened the drawer and inside he found a sheaf of papers. He rummaged around underneath and there he found a magnifying glass – and two gold medals. The room went quiet for several seconds.

Simon examined the medals and saw they were for the Leinster Senior Cup and the Bateman Cup, just as Eoin had said. Steve had no explanation for the medals being there and just shrugged when Simon told him he should leave the building right away and that he would be in touch with him later.

As soon as Steve had left Simon apologised to the boys and thanked them for helping expose the thief who may have stolen several items from the museum's collection already.

'I'm sorry, I shouldn't have sent you down to him, but I was very busy when you cornered me. We hadn't worked out who the thief was, though we knew an insider was involved. We believed someone on the staff was working with a gang of other men, some of whom were always calling in to check on how the museum was coming together. I'm very sorry to learn that it was Steve!'

'We'll let the Gardaí know what's been going on, but before that let's go back outside,' Simon said. 'People will be wondering what's going on. And don't you have a match to go to at some stage, Eoin?'

Eoin's mouth dropped wide open and he checked the time. 'I've got sixty seconds to get to the dressing room,' he gasped. 'Bye!'

And with that he ducked out the side door to the museum and hared off as fast as he could towards the grandstand. He had to explain he was a player to a couple of security staff, but got through and right to the door of the dressing room very little to spare.

Mr Carey was standing in the doorway, looking at his watch as Eoin arrived.

'I think I made it a little early,' Eoin said to the coach with a cheeky grin.

'Four seconds, Mr Madden, four seconds. You do believe in cutting things fine don't you. I hope the visit to the museum was worthwhile, now get in there and get kitted out – we've a job to do today.'

CHAPTER 43

Eoin's team-mates cheered when we walked into the dressing room.

'Sorry I missed dessert, lads,' he said, 'I had a museum opening to go to.'

'You missed nothing,' said Kieran. 'We got an apple or a banana. It's madness – you can't have a dessert without ice cream.'

There was a chorus of 'hear, hear' from the rest of the team, who were all togged out in their shiny new green and white hooped Castlerock shirts.

Eoin quickly changed into the match kit and sat on the bench tying his bootlaces. Ross Tierney came over and sat next to him.

'Are you in the zone, Eoin?' he asked. 'I'm not sure Johnny will be able to get through the whole game, so I need you to be ready to step up whenever you're called upon.'

Eoin nodded. 'I'm ready now,' he replied. 'I'm buzzing to get out there so whenever the team needs me, I'll be on my game.'

When the team filed out on to the playing pitch the stands were still empty, waiting for the supporters to arrive for the big game. Eoin smiled inside as he looked around the old ground that held many great memories for him.

He took an armful of balls away and began practising goal kicking. He kicked from wide out on the right towards the Havelock Square End and clipped the first two kicks over, but the third sliced away wide off the left-hand post. He strolled over to collect the ball when suddenly Brian appeared beside him.

'Hey, Eoin, do you see where that ball just landed? That's the spot where I was injured in my last game for Lansdowne, just in front of the West Stand. I sometimes come by here, but I try not to think about what happened, just about the great men I played alongside. I have such great memories of my playing days – I was never happier. I hope you are storing up rugby memories for when you get old and cannot play anymore.

'That's what's so good about that museum out the back. It does bring me back to watching those fantastic players over the years and all the excitement they brought to this stadium. I'm looking forward to going back there when its quieter and having a good look around.'

Eoin remembered Brian's crucial role in solving the crime.

'Thanks for letting me know about the medals being in the desk,' he told him. 'I was really afraid that thief was going to get away with it.'

Brian grinned. 'Yeah, I was keeping an eye on him all morning after George told me about him. It was so good to catch him in the act.'

'Did you see the medals were won by someone from Lansdowne – you probably played with him at some stage,' said Eoin.

'Yes, the Bateman Cup was a very big deal in those days, we had a particularly good side. I wasn't with the club when we first won it though,' replied Brian, 'And then when we next won I was six feet under.'

Eoin picked up the balls. 'I better get back to practice,' he said. 'They're going to think I'm a bit weird standing here talking to myself.'

He returned to his task, and by the time he was finished he was happy that he was in a good kicking groove. Johnny Costello came over and Eoin helped him practise by collecting the balls and returning them to him.

Johnny asked him a few questions about kicking in the stadium, of which Eoin had much greater experience.

'It's a strange ground to kick in sometimes,' Eoin told him. 'The wind sometimes swirls around at this end and can catch the ball and do funny things with it. It takes a while to get used to it, though it's not too windy today.'

CHAPTER 44

As kick-off time neared, Castlerock and St Malachy's returned to the arena and posed for team-group photos. Eoin stood near the edge of the back row, reluctant to push himself into the centre of the shot. He imagined being back there in two years, sitting in the middle of the front row with Dylan and Shane and all the other guys he had grown up with. He didn't really feel the team captained by Ross was 'his' team.

He pushed such negative thoughts to the back of his mind – he knew he could well have an important job to do today and needed to focus on that whenever he was called upon.

While the starting teams got into position for kick-off, he walked back to the bench. He looked up at the west stand and spotted a few of his pals among the spectators. He knew his parents, and grandad were there too.

His nerves started to wobble a bit at the thought of all those who were expecting him to be the hero. He noticed that there were a lot more Castlerock colours in the crowd. St Malachy's was a smaller school, to be fair, but had been in several finals in recent years – the Castlerock support included quite a lot of past pupils eager to see their school return to greatness.

Eoin took his seat beside Oisín and watched as Johnny kicked off towards the Lansdowne Road end. The wind whipped the ball away from the charging Castlerock forwards and flew straight into touch. Johnny held his head in his hands at the basic error as the forwards regrouped for a scrum on half-way.

St Malachy's pack were keen to show their power early in the game and having taken the heel their Number Eight picked up the ball as the maul drove forward. Castlerock struggled to keep them back, but their momentum was too great and they soon reached the 22-metre line.

Eoin watched with horror as the scrum-half took the ball from the maul and darted towards midfield. Kieran stood between him and the line, but the Castlerock man was just too slow reacting and the scrum-half sold him a dummy and scooted past him and raced for the posts. He touched down and leapt in the air with delight. The conversion was completed and the Castlerock supporters were stunned – less than two minutes gone, and they were already seven points behind.

Eoin looked across to where Mr Carey was sitting, and the coach's face was white with shock.

'Kieran's just not up for this,' whispered Oisín, 'he was a bad selection.'

Eoin just nodded, thinking it better not to saying anything until after he had played his own part in the day.

Ross gathered the team around him to delivering a passionate wake-up call. Eoin noticed that Kieran spent the whole talk staring at the ground, probably embarrassed that his mistake had cost the team so dearly.

Play resumed and Castlerock spent the next fifteen minutes in the opposition half without really threatening to score.

Eoin watched the opposition closely and realised that most of their backs were not very quick at all, and that although the forwards were powerful in the scrum and maul, their lineout jumpers weren't a patch on Ross and Keelan. As the half went on Castlerock won more and more possession and Johnny got them on the scoreboard with a penalty from just outside the 22 right before the half-time whistle.

Eoin walked back towards the dressing room, scanning the crowd as he went. He spotted his family in one of the boxes on the middle-deck of the stand, his mother waving down at him. Eoin raised his hand in salute and smiled at his parents.

In the dressing room there were loud voices everywhere, complaining about the opposition, the referee, and Kieran's missed tackle.

Ross held his hand up and called for silence.

CHAPTER 45

'That wasn't Castlerock out there,' Ross told his team. 'I don't know who it was, but it wasn't the team that beat Blackstones and St Osgur's.

'This is now a Mount Everest, boys. We've are going to have to play better than we have yet to get the top.

'St Malachy's don't respect you. They don't rate you. The only way to make them is to stick one on them, to get right up in their faces and turn them back, knock them back. Outdo what they do. Out-jump them, out-scrum them, out-ruck them, out-drive them, out-tackle them, until they're sick of you.

'Remember how you depend on each other at every phase, teams within teams, scrums, lineouts, ruck ball, tackles.

'They are better than any team we've played against so far. It's an awesome task you have now, and it will only be done if everybody commits himself now.

188

'If you put in the performance, you'll get what you deserve.'

There was absolute silence in the changing room for a few seconds before Johnny started to clap. Others joined in and soon there was cheering and shouting as if Castlerock had already won the game.

Eoin had felt a tingle run up his back as Ross was speaking. He looked around the room and thought each of the players looked six inches taller and much more up for the battle ahead than they had been before Ross opened his mouth.

Mr Carey said a few words too. He said he wouldn't make any changes just yet, but wanted the front row to push hard for the next twenty minutes.

Eoin nipped into the bathroom, as he had got into the habit of doing at half-time in big games. And, as usual, there was Brian waiting for him.

'Your team looks up against it,' the ghost told him. 'That other team are a tough bunch, very strong up front. And the Castlerock midfield is a bit of a mess — is the outside-half fully fit?'

Eoin shook his head and explained how Johnny was just back from injury. 'He has played very little this year but thought he was fit enough to play. I expect I'll be coming on at some stage — maybe for the last twenty minutes.'

Brian nodded. 'Have you noticed how slow their backs are, especially on the back foot. If you do get on maybe try a few kicks in behind them.'

'Thanks, Brian,' replied Eoin. 'The score is not too bad now, but I'd be afraid if we fell too far behind.'

Back in the dressing room the team were huddled in little groups talking to the various coaches. Mr Carey tapped Eoin on the shoulder.

'Are you ready, Eoin?' he asked. 'It depends on a few things, but I'd like to bring you on about ten minutes into the second half. Get yourself in the zone and start your warm-up when I give you a nod.'

When he got back on the bench Eoin re-tied his bootlaces and started his pre-match routine. Play kicked off and Castlerock looked still hyped-up after Ross's inspiring talk.

But a silly mistake by Anthony Morris, who went off-side at a ruck, gave St Malachy's a chance to extend their lead to 10-3 – which their full-back duly did.

Mr Carey looked along the bench and nodded at Eoin, who took it to mean he needed to get ready. He took off his tracksuit and jogged up and down the touchline before stopping in the in-goal area to do a few stretches and sprints. He jogged back to the bench where the coach told him he would be coming on at the next break in play. Oisín grinned up at him and wished him luck.

Sure enough, Johnny kicked the ball out of play and the touch judge signalled to the referee that a change needed to be made. Eoin started to run onto the field and ran towards Johnny to shake his hand when another of the Castlerock players stuck his hand out in front of him.

'Good luck, Eoin, hope you do a better job than me,' he said with a sigh. It wasn't Johnny he was replacing, but the inside centre, Kieran.

CHAPTER 46

Eoin didn't know where to go for a second or two, then he found his place in the backline and started to take stock. What on earth was Mr Carey doing? He had played centre only once before, back in First Year. He knew Kieran wasn't firing and he needed to be replaced, but Eoin expected that he would fill Johnny's place at out-half and was unsure of what exactly was expected of him at No.12.

'Hey, Eoin, good to see you,' said Johnny. 'We need a bit of inspiration at this stage. We haven't looked like scoring a try.'

Eoin shrugged his shoulders. 'I hope I can help, but to be honest I'm a bit lost about what I'm doing at centre.'

Johnny grinned back at him. 'You'll be grand. Just get your tackles in and be ready when I zing you a killer pass.'

Although they had been set back by the penalty goal,

Castlerock were showing signs of improvement from the first half. Ross kept quoting little lines from his speech to remind them of what they needed to do and the tactic seemed to be paying off. Johnny, too, was showing a bit more of the spark that made him such a good out-half.

Midway through the second half he went on a run, skipping in between the cover and darting into the opposition 22. Eoin stayed on his shoulder, ready to take a pass, and when the St Malachy's full-back cut Johnny off at the knees Eoin was there to collect his flip back. He pushed off his right leg and sprinted for the line, muscling through the tackles and stretching his arm out to ground the ball on the line.

The stadium erupted. Eoin heard his name being chanted by his school's supporters and he grinned as he watched the score change on the big screen to record 'Castlerock 8 St Malachy's 10'.

His team-mates slapped his back and ruffled his hair as he walked back, but it was only then that he noticed Johnny was still lying in the ground being attended by the school physio.

'I took a bad bang,' he told Ross. 'I think my knee has gone again.'

The physio nodded. 'Better tell Mr Carey he'll need

to be replaced.'

As Johnny was being helped from the field, his replacement Ethan Trehy came running up to Eoin.

'Coach says you're to slot in at 10, I'm playing centre,' he told him.

'Thanks, Ethan!' Eoin said, suddenly realising he would have to take the goal kicks too with Johnny out of action. He called for the kicking tee and took the ball back to where he reckoned was the best distance and angle for him.

He pulled up a few blades of grass and scattered them to check whether there was any wind. He then took a deep breath and checked his line before running at the ball. Another roar signalled the two extra points for Castlerock, which soon blinked onto the scoreboard showing the game was tied at 10-10.

Eoin moved back into the out-half slot for the restart, instantly feeling more at home than he had been at centre. He looked over his shoulder at Ethan, who gave him a nervous grin.

Castlerock had also brought on a new front row and the fresh blood was eager to make the most of their time on the pitch. They took control of the scrum, pushing hard against their tiring opponents. Soon, Castlerock were dominating position, and surely the scores would come now.

But St Malachy's were fighters and although they were under constant pressure they never cracked. Time was ticking away and still Castlerock could not find a breakthrough. Eoin looked up at the big screen and saw there was less than five minutes left.

During the next break in play Eoin called his team-mates into a huddle and explained the plan he had in mind. He suggested switching Ethan, who was a fast runner, out onto the wing.

Play restarted with a scrum and Castlerock won the heel. The scrum-half flicked the ball back to Eoin who remembered Brian's suggestion and immediately launched a kick into the left-corner. The St Malachy's defence was again slow to turn and by the time they had Ethan was haring towards the ball. He picked it up two metres short of the line and scampered over, cutting inside to give Eoin an easier angle on the conversion.

Eoin punched the air, delighted that his plan had come off, and grinned as the stadium erupted in a sea of green and white.

'Three minutes left,' said Ross as he tossed Eoin the ball. 'Take your time and get this right.'

Eoin stole a glance up to the stands where his family were seated, and smiled as Dixie raised his arm to him.

He switched back to the goalposts and prepared to kick. He spotted a lone figure with a black, red and gold hooped jersey standing behind the goal. The ghost pointed straight over his head.

Cheers, Brian, no wind, so! Eoin thought as he ran to kick the ball. Sure enough, the ball spun over the bar! Castlerock were now seven points to the good. There wasn't long left to prevent St Malachy's scoring, and the pack did their job until the referee sounded the final whistle.

'Wahoo!' Eoin roared, as the fourteen other men in green leapt around in delight. The substitutes raced on to join them and even Oisín and Johnny limped back towards the middle to take part in the fun.

CHAPTER 47

The players stayed on the pitch for ages, enjoying the moment and waving to their friends and family around the ground. They commiserated with St Malachy's, thanking them for a good game, and Eoin went over to the sideline to sign a few programmes for the Castlerock First Years.

'I'm Sam Farrelly's little brother,' said one of the boys as Eoin scribbled his name.

'Ah you're the famous Bobby,' he replied. 'I hope you're going to keep playing rugby. I hear you're really good.'

Bobby's smile widened, delighted that his hero had even heard about him.

Eoin chatted to a few of his pals until Mr Carey called them up to receive their medals and they all lined up in front of the West Stand.

They climbed the steps into the area where the

Leinster Rugby officials were waiting, along with Ross Tierney's mum. The long-standing tradition was that the captain's mother presented him with the prize and Mrs Tierney had a huge smile as she handed over the trophy.

Eoin collected his medal and climbed up to where his parents were watching.

'Fantastic play, Eoin,' said Dixie. 'That was very clever to chip the ball in behind the defence.'

Eoin smiled and grinned over to where Brian was standing.

'Yeah, it wasn't all my idea,' he replied. 'I did get a bit of help from one of my friends.'

His mother kissed his cheek and asked him would he be captain next year. 'I'd have to get a new coat if I have to present you with the cup,' she told him.

Eoin's father laughed and said if that was the case he would make sure Eoin twisted an ankle before he ever played in another Senior Cup final.

Alan and Dylan had followed Eoin up the stairs and the pair took turns to hug their pal.

'That was such class,' Dylan said, 'You just changed the game.'

Alan was carrying a large brown envelope which he handed to Eoin.

'Take a look what's inside there,' he said. 'After you rushed off I was flicking through the pile of photos that Dixie brought up for the Museum and I came across this.'

Eoin carefully opened the envelope, which was a black and white team group photograph taken in front of one of the old clubhouses he recognised from his book on the history of Lansdowne Road.

'Lansdowne RFC first XV, 1927-28' was written on the margin underneath. Eoin scanned the faces and immediately recognised the young man sitting on the ground at the front with his arms and legs crossed.

'Brian! That's Brian Hanrahan,' he told Dixie, showing him the photo. 'I remember you telling me about him, Grandad.'

Eoin noticed that Brian's ghost had moved around behind his grandfather to check out the photograph.

'Is this one of the photos I gave you for the museum?' Dixie asked.

'Yes,' replied Eoin. 'Alan recognised him. I suppose we really should give it back to the museum?'

'That would be nice,' said Dixie. 'It would be great to have him remembered in such a place. I'm sure he would have been happy to hear that if he was still around.'

Brian smiled and winked at Eoin, before he suddenly

disappeared.

'Where's he gone?' whispered Alan.

'There he is,' replied Dylan, pointing down to the pitch.

Eoin leant on the railing and looked down towards the Havelock Square End of the ground. There were two grown men running around like schoolboys, kicking an imaginary rugby ball and diving to catch it.

Eoin smiled and thought how happy George and Brian were to be back in a place they once played – and would always be remembered.

HISTORICAL NOTE

George Hall Stack was the first captain of the Ireland rugby team. He was from County Tyrone, but went to school in Donegal and to college in Dublin where he was very active in rugby circles. He hosted the meeting where it was decided to form the IRFU in his apartment in Trinity College. His only cap was in February 1875 at the Oval in London; he died in Dublin in November 1876, aged just twenty-six.

You can read more about the early days of Lansdowne Road in *Lansdowne Road: The Stadium; the Matches; the Greatest Days* by Gerard Siggins and Malachy Clerkin, published by O'Brien Press.

ALSO AVAILABLE

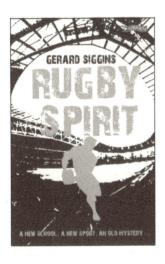

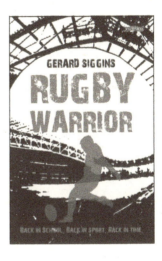

Eoin has just started a new school … and a new sport. Everyone at school is mad about rugby, but Eoin hasn't even held a rugby ball before! And why does everybody seem to know more about his own grandad than he does?

Eoin Madden is now captain of the Under 14s team and has to deal with friction between his friend Rory and new boy Dylan as they battle for a place as scrum-half. Fast-paced action, mysterious spirits and feuding friends – it's a season to remember!

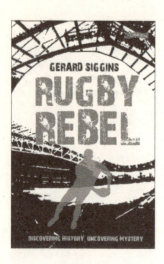

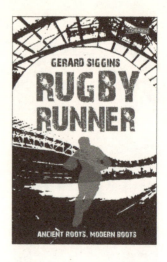

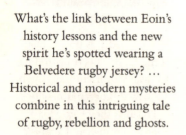

What's the link between Eoin's history lessons and the new spirit he's spotted wearing a Belvedere rugby jersey? … Historical and modern mysteries combine in this intriguing tale of rugby, rebellion and ghosts.

Eoin is captain of the Junior Cup team, training with Leinster and aiming for Ireland's Under 16 World Cup team. He also has to deal with a ghost on a mission that goes back to the very origins of the game of rugby.

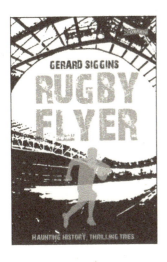

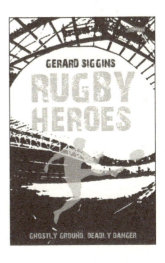

Eoin has been chosen for the Junior development squad so over the summer he gets to go to Dublin for a rugby summer school. But when his new friends are taken on a trip to Twickenham, London, to play and watch rugby there are ghostly goings on.

Eoin been called up for Ireland in the Under 16 Four Nations! When his oldest and best ghostly friend calls for help, can Eoin and his band of heroes solve their deadliest mystery yet

With no rugby over the summer, Eoin and his friends head to Ormondstown GAA club to get involved in hurling and football. Some local bullies spoil things a bit – but when the ghosts of Brian Hanrahan and Michael Hogan appear, it's clear there is something more sinister brewing.

Eoin wants a break from rugby this year and he jumps at the chance to play soccer instead! But who is the ghostly footballer with links to Dalymount Park that Eoin and his friends keep meeting? From Busby Babes to Castlerock Red Rockets, football links the generations.